Wakefie
& Informa

D0714601

This book should be returned by the last date stamped
above. You may renew the loan personally, by post or
telephone for a further period if the book is not required by
another reader.

About the author

Robert Rigby is best known for writing the bestselling *Boy Soldier* series with Andy McNab. He began his career as a journalist, then turned to writing for radio, television and the theatre and has also directed and performed in children's theatre throughout the country. He wrote the novelizations of the movies, *Goal!* and *Goal II*, and a third novel in the series, *Goal: Glory Days*. His scripts for television include the long-running BBC children's drama, *Byker Grove*.

ALSO IN THIS SERIES

Running in her shadow

Parallel lines

Wheels of fire

Deep waters

An official
London 2012 novel

Robert Rigby

CARLTON
BOOKS

First published by Carlton Books Limited 2011
Copyright © 2011 Carlton Books Limited

London 2012 emblems: ™ & ® The London Organising Committee
of the Olympic Games and Paralympic Games Ltd (LOCOG) 2007.
London 2012 Pictograms © LOCOG 2009. All rights reserved.

Carlton Books Limited, 20 Mortimer Street, London, W1T 3JW.

A CIP catalogue record for this book is available from the British Library.

10 9 8 7 6 5 4 3 2 1

ISBN: 978-1-84732-764-2

Printed in the UK by CPI Mackays, Chatham, ME5 8TD

One

For a split second, as she turned her head to the right to quickly suck in a breath, Lucy thought she saw another swimmer waving at her from across the pool. But then, concentrating on her training, she dipped her face back into the water and swam powerfully onwards.

The pool was quite crowded. Serious swimmers like Lucy were ploughing up and down in the marked-off lanes that were reserved for club members, while adults with children splashed about happily in the shallow end.

Two lifeguards were on duty, alert and watchful as ever. But at that moment their attention was grabbed by a couple of yelling teenage boys, who leapt into the water as close as they could to a group of girls, making them shriek and scream.

Lucy reached the end of the pool, touched the wall and turned to start another length. And then she spotted the swimmer again, and this time she realised instantly that he wasn't waving at all – he was drowning.

Scores of people were enjoying themselves in and around the pool, but in those vital seconds, only Lucy had noticed the man, who was in desperate trouble. She stopped swimming and glimpsed his panic-stricken face in the instant before he disappeared beneath the surface. And he didn't come up again.

Moving like lightning, Lucy dived down and swam underwater, her vigorous strokes and leg kicks taking her swiftly to the man, who had sunk to the bottom of the pool.

Lucy knew the basics of lifesaving, so she moved behind the man, put her arms under his armpits, made sure that she had a firm grip on his shoulders and then kicked off the bottom of the pool, sending them both upwards through the water.

As soon as they broke the surface, Lucy began to shout. 'Help! I need help here!'

A few people closest to Lucy heard the call, and the nearest lifeguard turned to look in her direction, just hearing Lucy's shout above the noise of the shrieking girls and yelling boys.

'Help!' Lucy shouted again, turning onto her back and kicking towards the side of the pool. She clutched the man tightly, keeping his head above the water, but it was hard work and exhausting. Lucy was fifteen and a powerful swimmer, but the man was much older, much bigger and unconscious. Lucy was swimming for them both.

'Help! Someone help me!'

This time, the lifeguard heard Lucy clearly and spotted the young swimmer towing the man towards the side of the pool. The lifeguard sprang into action, calling to his colleague and then diving into the pool. In seconds he was alongside Lucy and the unconscious swimmer. As Lucy panted for breath, the second lifeguard arrived and the two young men took over, using all their skills and strength to lift the other man carefully from the water.

Everyone was now staring towards the dramatic scene at the poolside and even the noisy boys and girls were stunned into silence.

The unconscious man lay completely still, his eyes closed and his face deathly pale. For a few terrifying moments, it seemed as though all Lucy's brave efforts had been in vain. Then suddenly he coughed twice, as though choking.

Lucy stared, her eyes wide. 'Please be all right,' she whispered. 'Please.'

The man's body jerked as he coughed again, bringing up much of the water he had swallowed. Spluttering and gasping for air, his eyes opened and the colour began to return to his cheeks. His eyes glazed and confused, he stared up at the two lifeguards kneeling at his side, 'Don't know what ... happened,' the man panted, fighting for breath. 'But thank you... Thank you so much.'

One of the lifeguards smiled. 'Don't thank us, mate,' he said, nodding towards Lucy. 'She's the one you should be thanking. She saved your life.'

Suddenly cheers and applause rang around the pool and everyone's eyes were on Lucy, who instantly felt her face blush bright red with embarrassment.

'What a hero!' someone shouted. 'That girl deserves a medal!'

Two

DISABLED SWIMMER MAKES HEROIC LIFESAVING RESCUE

Lucy scowled as she read the headline splashed across the front page of the newspaper.

'Why do they *always* have to start everything by saying that I'm disabled?' she said crossly. 'I'm a person; this makes me sound as though I'm different to everyone else.'

Lucy's dad, Tom, smiled as he settled onto the sofa. 'I suppose they think that because you have a disability what you did was even more amazing. And anyway, you *are* different to everyone else.'

'What do you mean?' Lucy said, frowning.

'You're special. You're *my* daughter and you're the best swimmer in the whole of Newham – and possibly the entire world. And it's lucky for the man you rescued that you are!' He took the newspaper from Lucy and studied the page. 'And that's a lovely photo of you, by the way. You look just like me!'

'*Dad*!' Lucy said, laughing. 'It's a horrible photo. And I only did what anyone else would have done. And don't forget, you've got *two* daughters.'

'Oh, I never forget that,' Tom answered proudly. 'And they're both equally special to me.' He pointed at the photograph in the newspaper. 'But my oldest daughter has become Lucy Chambers, the celebrity, over the past few days.'

Lucy sighed, realising that even though she found the situation highly embarrassing, her dad's words were more or less true. Since the dramatic rescue, the telephone had hardly stopped ringing. Everyone wanted to know more about Lucy Chambers. There had been radio and television interviews, newspaper articles and even a meeting with the Mayor of London. And it looked as though Lucy really would receive a medal for bravery.

It was all becoming too much. Lucy enjoyed seeing her name in the newspapers when she won a race or swam for the national team, but when it came to being a celebrity, she didn't like it. She was naturally shy and reserved, and being in the spotlight for anything other than swimming made her feel uncomfortable.

Lucy lived in Newham, East London with her dad, step-mum Jo and her step-sister Mia, who was ten.

Their terraced house was just a short distance from the London 2012 Olympic Park.

The family had watched excitedly as the Lower Lea Valley was transformed from a rundown area of waste ground and deserted factory buildings to a beautiful parkland dotted with trees and criss-crossed with walkways and the meandering River Lea.

Every time the Chambers family passed the site on the train it seemed to have changed a little more, but now the towering Olympic Stadium, the cycling Velodrome, the Handball Arena and the amazing Aquatics Centre were almost complete. The games would begin in less than a year.

The whole area was a magical sight, but it was the beautiful, wave-like, Aquatics Centre that fired Lucy's imagination most and set her heart thumping.

She longed to swim there and represent Great Britain in the 2012 Paralympic Games. And this wasn't just a distant dream but a strong possibility, as Lucy was already one of the top-ranking British Paralympic swimmers. Competition was fierce though and Lucy knew it was going to be a battle to make sure of her place.

Swimming was a massive part of Lucy's busy life. She trained for up to three hours every day, apart from Sundays, and then there was racing and travelling time on top. At school, Lucy was working hard towards her

GCSE exams so she also had to find time for lots of homework. There were barely enough hours in the day to do everything. And since the swimming-pool rescue, life had become even more hectic.

But now, as she watched her dad read the latest story about his daughter's bravery, Lucy decided that it was going to stop. 'I've had enough,' she said loudly.

He dad looked up from the newspaper.

'Enough what?' he asked.

'No more interviews. No more newspaper articles. I just want to get back to being me.'

'Fair enough,' her dad said. 'It's your life. You must decide what you want.'

'Exactly,' Lucy said, pleased that her dad agreed.

As Tom folded the newspaper, they heard the telephone in the kitchen start to ring.

Footsteps thundered down the stairs. Lucy grinned at her dad. They both knew that the footsteps came from Mia, who loved answering the telephone.

Moments later, the door opened and Mia came in carrying the handset. 'It's for you, Lucy,' she said sadly. 'It's always for you.'

'Who is it?'

Mia shrugged her shoulders. 'A reporter from the *Sunday* … something or other. I forget the name. But she said that she wants to write a story about you. Another one!'

Three

Lucy simply loved being in the pool. She loved the feel of the water and the way it parted for her as she swam, carving her way through like a speeding fish or a darting dolphin.

She loved everything about water. The way tiny bubbles bounced and swirled around her face as she swam; the way sound changed and became distant and ghostly when her head was beneath the surface; the way tiny, rippling waves cast dancing shadows on the tiles at the bottom of the pool. Lucy lived for swimming. Sometimes she thought she should have been a dolphin – her dream was to swim with dolphins.

But what Lucy loved most of all about water and swimming was that they made her disability almost disappear. Lucy had cerebral palsy, which affected the way she moved. It had been spotted when she was about two years old and as she grew older Lucy learned that she would never have full movement in her right arm and leg. There was a tightness that would not go away. The disability was noticeable when she walked, but in the water her movement was much freer and easier. It was her very favourite place to be.

Lucy was thinking just how good it felt to be in the pool and away from newspapers and the television as she neared the end of another training session. Her best events were the 200m and 400m Freestyle, so training often meant ploughing up and down the pool for length after length to build up her strength and stamina. But she never minded how many lengths she swam. Sometimes her coach, Dave Naylor, almost had to drag her from the pool.

'Okay, Lucy,' Dave shouted from the poolside as the young swimmer turned to start another length, 'two more and that's enough for today.' He smiled. 'Glad to see that being a celebrity hasn't affected your swimming too much!'

If Lucy hadn't been concentrating on her stroke, she would have stopped there and then to tell Dave that *nothing* was going to affect her swimming. She wouldn't allow it. Nothing was going to come between Lucy and her bid to make the London 2012 Paralympic team.

Lucy was going to swim for Great Britain in the wonderful Aquatics Centre.

She simply knew it.

No question.

No doubt.

A little later, Lucy was sitting at the poolside with her best friend Rose, who was a member of the same swimming club.

Training was over for them both, although Rose had climbed from the water much sooner than her friend. Rose was a good swimmer, but not international class like Lucy.

Rose didn't train very hard and wasn't too bothered about becoming a better swimmer. Lucy often thought that Rose's main reason for coming was to be with her friends – especially Lucy – because she seemed to lead quite a lonely life at home.

'Dad was going to come and collect me, but he sent a text earlier saying that he's working late and Mum is too,' she said to Lucy as she towelled her hair dry. 'So he asked if your dad would mind driving me home?'

Lucy smiled. Her own parents were used to giving Rose a lift home as it happened often. 'I'm sure that'll be fine,' she said. 'Dad won't mind at all.'

'They're always working late,' Rose said. 'I hardly ever see them. And when I do, all they ever talk about is work or how well James is doing at Uni.' She frowned. 'You're lucky that you haven't got an older brother –

especially one who's a lot cleverer than you are!'

Lucy laughed. 'I wouldn't mind a clever older brother; he could help me with my homework. I've got loads to do when I get home.'

'James never helps me,' Rose answered with a sigh. 'Whenever he's back from Uni, he's always out with his friends.' She looked very sad as she spoke.

Lucy found herself thinking how lucky she was to have such a loving family and settled home life. She smiled at her friend. 'Well, I'm really glad you'll be there to watch me swim in the match on Saturday. When I hear you cheering, it definitely makes me swim faster.'

Rose's face brightened. 'Oh, I'm great at cheering.' She grinned. 'And I'll make certain you hear me.'

Four

The noise was almost deafening. There was no way Lucy or any of the other swimmers could have picked out a single cheering voice. The sound echoed around the poolside and bounced down off the ceiling onto the churning water.

The spectators' gallery was crammed full. People were up out of their seats, yelling and shouting as the eight swimmers began their turns for the final 50 metres.

Lucy was tired. She could feel her strength beginning to drain away, but she was totally focused on making sure these were her best 50 metres of the day.

She was having a fantastic event. Swimming for the Great Britain Paralympic team brought out her very best. She had already won her group race in the 200m and now in the last race of the meeting, she was in third place. And there was very little between her and the leading two girls.

The home crowd yelled their support for Lucy. Leading the cheers and shouts of encouragement were her family and Rose.

'Come on, Lucy! You can do it!' yelled Tom, his deep voice booming down from the gallery.

'Go, Lucy, go!' screamed her mum, clenching her fists until her knuckles turned white.

Lucy's ears were filled with the sound of splashing water, but she knew her supporters would be shouting for her with every stroke she took, which was almost as good as hearing them. She also knew that her little sister, Mia, and Rose would be shouting louder than anyone around them.

And they were. 'Lu-cy! Lu-cy! Lu-cy! Lu-cy!' Rose and Mia chanted together, clapping their hands in rhythm with the word. 'Lu-cy! Lu-cy!' They were going to shout and clap their champion all the way to the finish.

Lucy took a breath, kicked away from the wall, and began her final surging sprint towards the finish. Her arms turned powerfully and her legs beat up and down, leaving a trail of bubbling water in their wake. She was moving fastest of all the swimmers and gaining quickly on the girl in second place.

'Lu-cy! Lu-cy! Lu-cy! Lu-cy!' Mia and Rose were so loud that other people around them began to join in. 'Lu-cy! Lu-cy! Lu-cy!

The next time Lucy snatched a breath, she actually heard her name – 'Lu-cy!' – and even though her arms were burning and her legs were aching, she was spurred on even more. She passed the girl in second place with 25 metres remaining.

'Lu-cy! Lu-cy!'

Another quick breath and Lucy battled on, closing on the leader with every stroke.

Even Tom and Jo had joined in the chant now. 'Lu-cy! Lu-cy!'

Ten metres, and Lucy was up alongside the leader, who seemed just as determined not to lose as Lucy was to win.

'Lu-cy! Lu-cy! Lu-cy! Lu-cy!'

Five metres and Lucy knew she had edged to the front. She powered on and reached for the wall, touching first by a fraction of a second.

The crowd roared, Jo and Tom hugged each other and Mia and Rose bounced up and down and gave each other high fives.

In the water, Lucy pulled off her goggles and turned to smile at the other girls who had all battled bravely to make it a fantastic race.

Up in the gallery, in one of the back seats, someone else was smiling proudly, her gaze fixed on Lucy. And as she turned away to leave ahead of the crowd, there were tears in her eyes.

It was Sunday, the day after the international swimming match. Sunday meant no training, so Lucy was enjoying a lazy day at home with her family. They had stayed in all day, glad that for once there was nowhere they needed to go and nothing that had to be done.

Lucy was tired but very happy. Her double success in the international match meant that she was a step closer towards making the 2012 Paralympic Swimming team. But for once, there was no talk of swimming or training. Everyone just made the most of a quiet, relaxing day.

Now, they were watching evening television and Lucy had already started thinking about the following day, which would mean early-morning training, school and then another training session.

Tom glanced at his watch and then at Mia. 'It's about time you were in bed, miss. School tomorrow.'

'Oh, Dad!' Mia complained. 'I love this programme; I watch it every week and I really want to see what happens next.'

Jo raised her eyebrows. 'Mia, I don't think you've ever seen this programme.'

'I *have*, Mum. And I always...' Whatever Mia was going to say about the programme was forgotten because the telephone had started to ring in the kitchen. 'I'll get it!' Mia yelled, leaping from her chair and running from the room before anyone else could move.

Tom smiled. 'I thought she didn't want to miss what happens next.' He looked over at Lucy. 'It's bound to be for you. Another celebrity interview maybe?'

Lucy snuggled further down into her chair. 'We'll, I'm not in.'

Moments later, Mia returned to the room and held out the telephone to her dad. 'For you,' she said.

'Who is it?' whispered Tom.

Mia frowned, trying to remember the name she had been given, but it had already slipped from her memory. She put the telephone to her ear. 'Who is it?' she asked and then nodded as the caller spoke.

'It's Sarah,' Mia said. 'Sarah Hammond.'

Tom's eyes widened and he turned to his wife, who looked just as startled. Then Tom stood up, took the telephone from Mia and walked from the room, closing the door behind him.

Five

'That woman is not coming back into our lives,' Tom said furiously. 'Not now and not ever.'

'It's not quite as simple as that, Tom,' Jo said calmly. 'And there's no point in getting angry and upsetting yourself. It won't help the situation at all.'

Tom had spent about five minutes on the phone. At first, the rest of the family heard nothing of the conversation, but then his voice became louder and louder, until finally he was shouting. And then suddenly everything went silent.

When Tom came back into the room his face was like thunder. 'Bed, Mia,' he said sharply.

'Oh, Dad...'

'*Now!*' Tom snapped.

Tom hardly ever got angry with his daughters, but when he did, they both knew not to argue.

'I'll come up and say goodnight in a little while,' said Jo.

'It's not *my* fault Dad had a horrible phone call,'

said a sad-faced Mia as she plodded from the room. She closed the door behind her.

Jo looked at her husband. 'She's right, you know.'

Tom nodded, but said nothing. He stared towards the window, taking deep breaths as though he were deliberately trying to contain his fury.

Lucy looked from one parent to another. 'Will someone please tell me what's going on? Who is this Sarah Hammond?'

For a moment no one spoke, but then Tom turned and nodded to Jo, as if he couldn't bring himself to mention the name again.

Jo sighed. 'Sarah Hammond is your … your natural mother. Hammond was her name before she married your dad. She went back to it after they were divorced.'

Lucy stared. 'Oh,' was all she could manage to say.

And that was when Tom, unable to contain his anger any longer, said furiously that 'that woman' would never be allowed back into their lives.

As Jo urged Tom to stay calm, Lucy's thoughts were racing. She had known for a long time that her natural mother, her dad's first wife, was called Sarah. But that was about as much as she knew and as much as she wanted to know, because as far as Lucy was concerned, Jo was her mum.

Lucy didn't remember Sarah at all, but learning so suddenly that she had been speaking on the phone to her dad just a few minutes before made her feel strange. Dizzy. Her head buzzed, as though blood were rushing wildly through her brain. Suddenly, she became aware of her dad's angry voice saying, '… walked out on us like she did and now she thinks she can just walk back in again. Well, she can't. I won't allow it. No way.'

'It isn't entirely up to you, Tom,' Jo answered sharply. 'And you're not the only one affected by this. I'm not exactly delighted that Sarah's chosen to make contact. But she has, and we always knew it was a possibility. So now it's up to Lucy to decided whether or not she wants to meet her … mother.'

'*You're* my mother,' Lucy said quickly. 'You always have been and you always will be.'

'Yes, I'm your mum,' Jo replied. 'But we can't pretend that Sarah doesn't exist.'

'Why not?' Tom said, his face still flushed with anger. 'She pretended we didn't exist for long enough. Now she sees Lucy's photo in the paper and suddenly she wants to know her famous daughter.'

'Is that it?' Lucy asked. 'Is that what she said?'

'No, not exactly,' Tom admitted. 'She *said* that she's wanted to make contact for years – to meet you and get to know you – but she's been too afraid to do it in case you rejected her. She *said* that seeing you in the paper finally made her mind up. But why should we believe her?'

'Because it's probably true,' Jo said. 'I can't imagine what it must have been like for her all these years, missing out on her daughter growing up.'

'It was her decision to walk out on Lucy and me,' Tom said.

'And maybe she regrets that decision now.'

'Well, it's too late for regrets.'

Jo nodded. 'But it's not too late for Lucy to meet her mother.' She paused for a moment and then looked at Lucy. 'If that's what you want.'

Tom turned to Lucy. 'Is it?' he asked. '*Is* that what you want?'

Lucy suddenly felt panicky. Both parents were looking at her, both waiting for her answer. 'I don't know,' she said. 'Honestly, I don't know.'

Six

Training wasn't proving easy because – for maybe the first time ever – Lucy wasn't focused on what she was doing. Her thoughts were somewhere else completely.

Ever since the conversation with her mum and dad the previous evening, she had been thinking about the person who wanted to come back into her life – her natural mother.

Over the years, Lucy had thought about Sarah only rarely. And when she thought about her natural mother, Lucy felt a mixture of sadness and anger that Sarah had left her when she was so young.

The sadness and anger never lasted for very long, though. Lucy was a naturally happy person and greatly loved by her family. So she never felt that she'd missed out on anything by not having Sarah in her life.

But now, after the phone call, Lucy suddenly realised that she wanted to know much more about Sarah. She had never even seen a picture of her. Were there any photos at home, hidden at the back of a cupboard or lying, fading and forgotten, in a box in the loft? If there were photos, Lucy wanted to see them. But she didn't dare ask her dad.

There was so much she needed to discover – simple things like the colour of Sarah's hair. Were her eyes pale blue, like Lucy's? And was Sarah tall, like Lucy? Did they look alike? And what about the sound of her voice? Did she have an accent? What sort of clothes did she wear? What did she like, and dislike? And was she a good swimmer, like her daughter? Suddenly there were so many questions – and Lucy wanted the answers.

But Lucy still couldn't answer the most important question of all – did she want to meet her mother or not?

Her mother.

Lucy still found it strange to think that she had any other mother than Jo. But she did. Sarah was her mother, too.

Thoughts and questions had been churning through her mind all day and they were still there as she swam that evening, and this was why she wasn't training properly.

'All right, Lucy, let's call it a day, eh?' her coach called from the poolside. 'You're not swimming well tonight; it must be because you're still tired from the races at the weekend.'

Lucy turned and swam, more slowly now, back up the length of the pool, easing the pace so that her muscles gradually relaxed. She touched the far side, rolled over onto her back and kicked gently, swimming without using her arms at all. As she glided leisurely down the lane, she stared upwards, watching the shimmering reflections the rippling water made on the ceiling.

Usually, when Lucy had something on her mind, just being in the water and letting it wash over her as she swam helped to clear her head and sort out her worries. But it wasn't working this evening. She felt totally muddled and confused.

Dave waited until Lucy came alongside and then smiled down at her. 'Something on your mind, is there?' he asked as Lucy stood up in the water and took off her goggles. 'Because you weren't thinking about swimming, that's for sure.'

'Sorry, Dave,' Lucy said. 'I'm a bit behind with some of my schoolwork. I need to catch up tonight.'

Lucy was telling the truth. She had slipped behind with a couple of subjects at school and she did need to make up the work. But that wasn't the real reason for her lack of focus. She didn't want to mention her worries to Dave. Not yet. Not before she had sorted out in her own mind what she was going to do. And not before she had talked her decision through with her family.

'Do you want to give tomorrow morning's session a miss?' Dave asked as Lucy climbed from the pool. 'Or you can skip both sessions if you really need the break. Sometimes it's not a bad thing, especially if you come back refreshed.'

'No, I'll be fine tomorrow,' Lucy said. 'Thanks for the thought though, Dave.' She smiled. 'You're not such a slave-driver after all.'

Dave grinned. 'Well, make sure you catch up with that schoolwork tonight or I'll make you swim an extra ten lengths tomorrow – at double speed.' He threw Lucy a towel and winked. 'See you in the morning.'

Rose was sitting on a bench in the changing room. As usual, she had finished the training session early and was already dressed and ready to leave when Lucy came in.

Lucy saw instantly that her friend was upset. 'What's wrong, Rose?' she asked gently.

Rose shrugged her shoulders. 'Everything?' she said. 'Or just about everything, anyway.'

Lucy was used to her friend's worries and knew that often they weren't nearly as bad as Rose imagined. But this time she really did look upset.

'Do you want to tell me about it?' Lucy asked.

Rose nodded. 'James is coming home from Uni at the weekend.'

'That's good, isn't it?'

'Normally it would be okay,' Rose said. 'But this time he's bringing his new girlfriend.'

'So what's wrong with that?'

'Mum says that she's got to have my bedroom because it's bigger and nicer than the spare room. It's just not fair!'

Lucy was almost always bright and happy and tried to see the best in every situation. Rose could be just as bright, and very funny, but when something went wrong, she sometimes decided that the whole world had turned against her. So Lucy often found herself having to cheer up her friend. It took a lot of patience, but fortunately Lucy had plenty of patience.

'It's just for a couple of nights, and it'll be great to meet James's girlfriend,' Lucy said. 'What's her name?'

Rose shrugged again, as though she couldn't care less what James's girlfriend was called. 'Vicky,' she said sulkily. 'I think.'

'I'm sure she'll be really nice,' Lucy said brightly. 'James is nice. He's bound to have a nice girlfriend.'

'Well, it's not just that,' Rose said quickly.

'What else is wrong?' Lucy asked, knowing that Rose's problems usually came in twos or threes.

Rose sighed. 'I bought myself some new jeans with the birthday money Gran gave me and Mum says I've got to take them back because they were too expensive. She says that I should save the money. But it's my money and I should be allowed to do what I want with it.'

Lucy was desperate to get changed. She was beginning to feel cold and was starting to shiver, but Rose looked *so* miserable. She tried again. 'Maybe you could save some of the money and swap the jeans for a pair that are not quite so expensive?'

'But I like the ones I've got. And anyway, Mum's been really horrible to me lately. Just because my school report wasn't great, she says that I might have to have extra maths lessons at home, which would be *horrible*. And it's not *my* fault that I'm no good at maths. It's just too hard.'

'Oh, *Rose*!' Lucy snapped. 'Will you please stop complaining!'

Rose wasn't used to Lucy raising her voice and she just stared.

But Lucy wasn't finished. 'You keep moaning about everything. Don't you ever stop to think that other people have worries, too – worries that might be much more serious and important than your silly little problems about spare rooms and new jeans?'

'But... But...'

Lucy grabbed her towel and stomped off towards the showers. 'Just for once, why don't you stop complaining and think about someone else, please?'

There were tears in Rose's eyes. 'Lucy!' she called. 'I'm sorry!'

Seven

Sarah Hammond was very like her daughter. Not only did they look alike – with the same colour eyes and hair – they were also both tall and slim. But the similarities didn't end there, because just like Lucy, swimming was a huge part of Sarah's life too. She worked as a swimming instructor and lifeguard on a cruise ship. And although her job took her all over the world, Sarah's home was in West London.

When she was at home, Sarah swam most days at the pool close to her small flat in Putney. Just like Lucy, she found that the swimming pool was the best place to think through her worries and problems.

It was two days since her phone call to Tom – and Sarah was in the pool. She was thinking, for the hundredth time about what had been said during their brief conversation and wondering and worrying about what might happen next.

Would Lucy want to meet her after all these years? Sarah desperately hoped she would, but in her heart she feared that Lucy would simply say, 'Why should I ever want to meet someone who left me when I was a baby and has never contacted me since?' This was perfectly true. Sarah *had* left her husband and little daughter. But for years she had dreamed of meeting Lucy and explaining how and why it had happened.

Sarah had searched so hard to find the right words. And when she had finally settled on them, she said them to herself, over and over, practising, imagining that Lucy was listening. Listening and then forgiving.

As Sarah swam that afternoon, she could hear the familiar words of explanation in her mind. 'I was so young. Your dad and I were both so young. We weren't ready to have a baby – we had no idea what it would be like. And then after you were born, I just couldn't cope... It all got too much. There was no one I could talk to and ... I didn't really want to run away, but...'

Sarah stopped swimming and stood up in the water. 'It sounds terrible,' she said out loud, realising that she had started to cry. As she wiped away the tears, she felt an arm around her shoulder and she turned. Her friend, Jill, was standing next to her.

Jill knew all about Sarah's attempt to make contact with her daughter and she knew how much it was worrying her friend. 'What is it?' she asked gently.

'I keep going over and over what I want to say to

Lucy,' Sarah said tearfully. 'But it's just an excuse – a *terrible* excuse – and there is no excuse for what I did. Lucy will never forgive me.'

'You don't know that,' Jill said. 'Look, how about we stop swimming for today? Let's get changed and go somewhere quiet where we can chat.'

As far as Jo Chambers was concerned, she had two daughters and she felt exactly the same about them both – she loved them completely. The fact that she had given birth to Mia and not to Lucy made absolutely no difference at all. They were both her girls.

But now the moment that Jo had always expected and secretly feared had finally arrived – Lucy's natural mother had returned.

And Jo was scared. She had never met Sarah Hammond; she hadn't even seen a photograph of her. When Jo first met Tom, he told her that he'd cleared his home of every trace of his first wife, even their wedding photographs.

But somewhere in the background Sarah had always been a part of Jo's life – a shadowy figure from Tom and Lucy's distant past who might one day return. And now that she had returned, there was no way of knowing what would happen.

Today, Jo and Mia were doing the weekly shop at a huge supermarket in Newham. Since Sarah's phone call, Mia had had plenty of questions for the rest of her family, particularly her mum.

'So will I see Lucy's other mummy, too?' Mia asked.

'I don't know, darling,' Jo replied. 'We don't even know if Lucy is going to see her.'

'Lucy won't go and live with her other mummy, will she?'

'Of course not. She might visit her sometimes. Perhaps. We don't know yet.'

'Oh.'

They reached the end of one aisle and turned into the next.

Mia looked thoughtful. 'Why did Lucy's other mummy run away from Daddy and Lucy?'

Jo reached for a packet of pasta and dropped it into the trolley. 'I don't really know, darling.'

Mia sighed. 'You always say that you don't know.'

Jo brought the trolley to a standstill and took one of Mia's hands in hers. 'I know I do, and I'm sorry. But the truth is that I really don't know why she left or what's going to happen now that she's returned. We're all going to have to wait and see.'

Mia thought for a moment and then nodded, looking very confused. 'Can I have some sweets, please? Fruit pastilles?'

Sarah and her friend Jill were having a cup of tea in the swimming pool's cafeteria. It was busier than either of them would have liked, but they had found a corner table and were chatting quietly.

'Perhaps I shouldn't have made contact at all,' Sarah said. 'Perhaps it was too selfish of me and I should have left them alone to get on with their lives. I imagine the whole family is upset now.'

'Probably,' Jill answered. 'A little. But Lucy has every right to see you, if she wants to.'

'I'd never insist on seeing her,' Sarah said quickly. 'I know that it's up to her. And I *will* understand if she says that she never wants to see me or hear from me again. It's just that it would … break my heart.'

Sarah took a sip of tea, knowing that she was close to tears again. Then she reached into her bag, unzipped an inner pocket and took out a small, faded colour photograph of a baby. She passed it over to her friend.

'That's Lucy when she was four months old. It was taken just before … just before I left. I always have it with me.'

Jill smiled as she looked at the photograph. 'She does look like you. Same eyes, same smile.'

'We didn't know about the cerebral palsy then. That wasn't why I left them.'

'I know,' Jill answered kindly. 'You don't have to explain.'

'But I want to,' Sarah said. 'And I have to explain to Lucy too. I want her to understand. I was so unhappy and I didn't know why. No one told me that it sometimes happens to a mum after her baby is born. It got worse and worse and I felt so alone.'

'And none of your own family was around to help?'

'My parents lived in Exeter, hours and hours away. Tom and I met when I was at college here in London. I didn't have any real friends here, and no family at all.'

'You must have felt terribly lonely.'

Sarah nodded. 'I said that I'd go back home to Exeter, just until I felt better. Tom agreed, and his mum and sister were happy to help with Lucy for a while. But I didn't feel better, not for a long time, and then, when I did, it was … it was…'

'Too late?' Jill asked gently.

'Tom said that they didn't want me any more; they didn't need me. At first I didn't believe him. I thought that he would still want me back, however long it had been. But he was so hurt after I'd abandoned them like that. And then I was too … ashamed of what I'd done to try to make him change his mind.'

'Perhaps you will get a chance to talk it through with Lucy,' Jill said.

'That's all I want,' Sarah said quickly. 'A chance to explain and then … who knows? I left Tom my mobile number and he said that he'd written it down. Now every time the phone rings or I get a text, I think that it might be Lucy, but so far…' She sighed. 'I'm trying hard to be patient.'

'You've waited all these years,' Jill said with a smile. 'You'll manage to wait just a little longer.'

Jo was loading the heavy shopping bags into the back of the car while Mia watched, sadly popping the last of her fruit pastilles into her mouth. It was red, her favourite colour; she always saved a red one until last.

'Mum?' she said, as she tried desperately not to chew the pastille so that it would last for as long as possible.

'Mmm?' Jo answered, packing another bag into the boot.

'I was thinking.'

'What about?'

'About Lucy's other mummy leaving Lucy and Daddy.'

'Oh. And what about it?'

Mia sucked gently on the pastille. It was getting smaller and smaller on her tongue. 'I'm glad she left them.'

Jo loaded the last bag, shut the boot and turned to her daughter. She smiled. 'And why is that, miss?'

'Well,' Mia said, 'if she hadn't left, then you wouldn't have got married to Daddy and then you wouldn't have had me.'

Jo laughed. 'You're absolutely right,' she said. 'And where would any of us be without you? Come on, jump in the car.'

She opened the passenger door and Mia climbed in, settled into the seat and smiled up at her mum. Then she frowned as she realised that the pastille had disappeared. The door clicked shut and Mia found herself wondering why the very nicest things couldn't last for ever.

Eight

When it was discovered that Lucy had cerebral palsy, the doctors told her dad that swimming might help her condition, so Tom made sure that his daughter got used to the water when she was still a toddler.

Lucy loved it from the very first time Tom carried her into the pool, and her passion for swimming and being in water had grown stronger and stronger.

But it was watching other disabled swimmers competing at the Beijing 2008 Paralympic Games that completely changed the way Lucy thought about swimming. Almost overnight, she went from being someone who enjoyed swimming to someone who was totally determined to reach the very top as a Paralympian.

Lucy was glued to the TV screen as she watched Liz Johnson – who also had cerebral palsy – win gold in the 100m Breaststroke. 'Go on, Liz! Go on, Liz!' she screamed, as though Liz were her best friend.

And she cheered and yelled as other British Paralympians swam to glory and then proudly received their medals.

But Lucy's loudest cheers were for Ellie Simmonds, who was just thirteen when she won two gold medals at Beijing 2008. Lucy decided that Ellie was totally inspirational to every person with a disability. She swam with amazing determination and courage, and in television interviews after her victories, she smiled and laughed and cried with joy, capturing the hearts of millions of TV viewers back in the UK and around the world.

Ellie was voted the Young Sports Personality of the Year and went to Buckingham Palace to be presented with an MBE by the Queen.

It was Eliie Simmonds who, more than anyone else, had inspired Lucy to strive to become a Paralympian and to strike for gold at London 2012.

Part one of the dream had been already achieved by representing Britain, but there was still much to do if Lucy was going to make the ParalympicsGB team and achieve her ultimate goal of a gold medal. So Lucy had decided that there was no rush to think about whether or not to meet Sarah Hammond. For now she would focus on her swimming and the London 2012 Games.

Lucy could only think of her natural mother as Sarah Hammond, not as 'Mum' – Mum was Jo – and certainly not as 'Mother'. Lucy couldn't think of *anyone* as Mother; it was a word she just wouldn't use. So for now it had to be 'Sarah Hammond' and for now Lucy wasn't going to rush into making a decision about seeing her. This was too important to rush.

And besides, Lucy kept reminding herself, London 2012 was getting closer by the day. She couldn't allow this confusing new situation to spoil her preparations and ruin her dream.

Lucy was at the pool for an event she always looked forward to – the club's own championships. But she was frowning as her eyes scanned the crowded poolside. Rose hadn't turned up, just as Lucy had feared. When she had emerged from her shower after the argument, Rose had already left for home. And there hadn't been a chance to speak since then.

Lucy walked towards one end of the pool for the start of her race, telling herself that tomorrow she must put things right with her friend. Then suddenly she felt annoyed with Sarah Hammond. Lucy didn't want to have negative thoughts before a race, but she couldn't stop herself from thinking that if it hadn't been for Sarah Hammond, she would never have had the row with Rose.

Clicking her tongue in irritation, Lucy told herself that she wasn't going to let Sarah spoil things with her friends and family or with her race that evening. Club members were racing against each other. It was a fun event, but it helped the swimmers to sharpen their racing technique, so the races were all fiercely fought.

And as there were no other members of the club with a disability similar to Lucy's, she was lining up against seven non-disabled swimmers in the 100m Freestyle race.

Lucy loved any competition and every challenge. There were several girls in the race with personal-best times equal to or better than hers, so winning would be tough. But Lucy was smiling as she climbed onto the starting block – she loved nothing more than a tough race.

'Take your marks!'

The poolside chatter quickly faded to silence and the eight swimmers crouched, staring down into the shimmering water. Then a short blast on a whistle sent them plunging into the pool.

Lucy's start was good and she was quickly up and into her stroke as cheers and shouts echoed around the building, bouncing off the huge windows and the ceiling.

Dave was with the other coaches; where all eyes were fixed on the young swimmers in their charge.

At the halfway point, Lucy was amongst the leaders. She turned, kicked away from the wall, glided beneath the surface like a dolphin and then went smoothly back into her stroke.

All the swimmers were being urged on, but the loudest cheers seemed to be for Lucy, who was probably the most popular swimmer in the entire club.

Over the final few metres, it looked as though any of the three or four leading girls could get the winning touch. In a flurry of whirling arms, kicking feet and splashing water they stretched and touched the wall almost as one.

Then, as the cheers died away, the eight girls turned and smiled, laughing and congratulating each other on a great race.

'I think I got it,' said one swimmer.

'No, I did,' said another.

'It was me,' claimed a third.

'No, I won,' said Lucy, laughing.

It had almost been a blanket finish, but the watching coaches finally decided that Lucy had finished in second place, beaten by a swimmer who had a faster personal-best time by the tiniest margin. Everyone said that it had been a terrific race and great fun. Nobody cared too much who had won.

Lucy climbed from the pool and went to speak to Dave, but before they had exchanged more than a few words, a group of younger swimmers came over and asked if they could talk to her.

Dave laughed. 'We'll speak later,' he said to Lucy. 'I'll leave you to your fan club for now.'

The youngsters began to chatter excitedly, most of them speaking at the same time and all of them telling Lucy that she had definitely won the race and that the coaches had got the result completely wrong.

Lucy felt a warm glow as she listened, realising that in less than four years she had gone from fun swimmer to top swimmer. And now it seemed that she too – like Ellie Simmonds – was becoming something of an inspiration to other youngsters. It made her feel a little embarrassed, but also quite proud.

'Do you think we should all complain, Lucy?' asked one girl very seriously.

'Complain?' said Lucy. 'What for?'

'If we complain that they got the result wrong, then they might make you the winner after all.'

Lucy laughed. 'But I didn't win!'

The swimming fans chattered on and Lucy found herself thinking that she probably wouldn't meet Sarah Hammond after all. She loved her life just the way it was. Why change things and risk spoiling it?

Nine

Lucy and Rose had made up.

First Lucy said that she was sorry. Then Rose said that she was sorry. Then each said that they were the most sorry. And then they started to laugh and things were swiftly back to normal.

Saturday-afternoon training was underway and as it was the weekend the pool was busier than on weekdays. Three lanes were reserved for club swimmers and were kept separate from the rest of the pool by a line of floats stretching from one end to the other. It meant that there was less room for the fun swimmers, but most of the regular pool users were used to seeing serious swimmers in training and didn't mind at all.

Lucy was midway through a 500-metre sequence and Rose was standing in the water watching, counting off the laps. Dave had been unable to make it to the session and Rose was enjoying pretending to be a trainer for the day.

'Keep it up, Lucy. Long steady strokes!' she called, trying to sound like Dave as her friend swam by. 'Nice rhythm now and no slacking.'

Lucy couldn't stop herself from laughing as she grabbed a breath and almost swallowed a mouthful of water.

Up in the viewing gallery, friends and relatives of the swimmers were watching. And one of them was Sarah Hammond.

Sarah had waited for days, as patiently as she could, for a call or a message from Lucy, or even from Tom. But when nothing happened she'd decided to make a move. She *had* to see Lucy again. She wasn't going to try to speak to her daughter, just to see her again for a little while would be enough. That was what she told herself when she decided that she would watch Lucy train. And as Sarah stared down at the pool, she couldn't quite hear what Lucy's friend was saying but she could hear the laughter and was glad to see the girls enjoying themselves.

Lucy could hear Rose loud and clear.

'You're really not going fast enough!' Rose barked in her very best Dave voice. 'You'll never make the Paralympic Games unless you go faster! Much faster!'

It was too much for Lucy. She laughed out loud as she took a breath and this time she did swallow a mouthful of water. Coughing and spluttering, she stopped swimming, struggled to her feet and pulled off her goggles.

'Rose!' she said, pretending to be angry. 'How am I supposed to train when you keep making me laugh?'

'Me?' Rose answered innocently. 'I'm not making you laugh. I'm just trying to make you work harder. Like Dave would.'

Lucy giggled and playfully ran her open hand across the surface of the water, sending a jet of water straight into Rose's face. Rose shrieked and splashed Lucy back and both girls were soon sweeping and flicking showers of water over each other, laughing and screaming in delight.

Suddenly, a man on the other side of the lane markers stopped swimming, stood up and glared angrily at the two girls. 'Would you please stop that!' He was almost shouting.

The two girls were having so much fun that for a moment they didn't hear the man.

'*Stop it!*' This time the man did shout and Lucy and Rose stopped their game and turned to look at him. He was red-faced with anger. 'It's bad enough that we have to give up part of the pool to you so-called *serious* swimmers, but if all you can do is mess about and behave like infants, then I shall ask the manager to throw you out!'

Lucy was ready to ignore the man and return to her swimming, but Rose spoke up for her. 'My friend happens to be a *very* serious swimmer. And she's almost definitely going to represent Great Britain in the Paralympic Games next year.'

The man glared at Lucy. 'Oh, I see. That's why you get the special treatment, like marked-off lanes,' he sneered. 'And I suppose you want us all to feel sorry for you? Well, I'm afraid that I don't. And why should I? I've got problems of my own.'

Lucy's eyes blazed with fury. 'I don't want you to feel sorry for me. I don't need anyone to feel sorry for me. In fact, I feel sorry for you!'

'Me!' the man gasped. 'And why should you feel sorry for me?'

'Because you have a real problem with your attitude.'

'What do you mean by that?' the man snarled.

In the viewing gallery, Sarah had left her seat and moved closer. She could hear every word that Lucy and the man had said to each other and was tempted to leap to her daughter's defence. But Lucy didn't need any help; she was managing perfectly well on her own.

'Anyone who talks about disabled people the way you do has a serious problem,' Lucy went on. 'Do you know something? You're a lot more disabled than I am – you're offensive.'

The man turned crimson with embarrassment. 'I only said that you get special treatment!' he blustered. 'This is a public pool. I've got my rights, too.'

Lucy had no intention of letting him get away with his remarks. 'Yes, but the real difference between us,' she said fiercely, 'is that I can't do anything about my disability, but you can do something about yours. I'm disabled for life. You don't have to be offensive for ever. So if I were you, I'd try to change while you've still got the chance!'

With that, Lucy turned her back on the man and smiled sweetly at her friend. 'Shall I carry on with my lengths now, Rose?'

Rose just stared in awe and nodded as Lucy replaced her goggles, dipped under the water and swam powerfully away.

The man's face was an even deeper shade of red. 'I ... I'm sorry,' he mumbled to Rose before turning away.

Sarah had seen and heard the whole incident and was almost glowing with pride. Watching her daughter stand up for herself so bravely and strongly had been like seeing her young self from afar. But her thoughts were suddenly interrupted as she heard footsteps running down the gallery stairs towards her. She turned to see a furious-looking man approaching.

'I thought it was you!' the man shouted. 'How dare you turn up here! How dare you!'

'Oh,' Sarah said quietly. 'Hello, Tom.'

Ten

Before swimming away from the man, Lucy had pulled on her goggles so quickly that she hadn't fitted them properly. And as she powered down the pool, water seeped through tiny gaps and got into her eyes.

When she finished the length, she stopped to refit the goggles. Pulling them from her head, she blinked to clear her eyes and then turned around to see if the man was still talking to Rose. He had disappeared amongst the other swimmers, but Lucy noticed that that her friend was now staring upwards, wide-eyed.

Lucy followed Rose's gaze and then gasped in horror at what she saw. Her dad was in the spectators' gallery, shouting at a woman and furiously jabbing his finger towards her as he spoke.

Behind them, further up the stairs, stood Jo and Mia, who were holding hands tightly. They both looked as upset as the woman at the receiving end of Tom's anger.

'Sarah Hammond,' Lucy whispered. 'It's Sarah Hammond.'

For a moment, Lucy didn't know what to do. She shivered, suddenly cold with fear; it was almost as though the water she stood in had turned to ice.

'Stop it, Dad,' she said softly, knowing that at this distance he couldn't possibly hear her. 'Please stop.'

Lucy had never seen her dad look so angry. Quickly, she swam across the pool to the ladder and climbed from the water.

All around, people were staring. In the water, at the poolside, in the gallery, every face seemed to have turned towards the scene that was unfolding.

'Dad!' Lucy called stumbling slightly as she got closer. She was trying to walk too quickly and suddenly became aware of her disability. 'Please stop shouting. You're upsetting Mum and Mia, and you're upsetting me, too.'

Tom looked back and saw that Mia was crying. He turned back to Sarah, angrier than ever. 'See!' he yelled. 'Do you see what you're doing and the trouble you're causing by turning up like this?'

Sarah looked at Lucy. For a fleeting moment, their eyes met.

'Lucy…' Sarah whispered.

'Get out!' Tom shouted. 'Clear off and leave us alone. You only want to know Lucy now she's famous! What happened to all the other years? Well, she doesn't want you. Nobody wants you. So just go, will you? Go!'

Lucy saw tears fill Sarah's eyes. Then without another word, the mother she had never really known turned away and ran up the stairs, past Tom, past Jo and Mia and out through the door.

And as Lucy stood shivering at the poolside, she felt her own tears streaming down her face.

It wasn't the best day to be driving Rose home. No one in the car had uttered a word since Tom pulled out of the car park in the pouring rain.

Jo sat next to her husband in the front and Mia was between Lucy and Rose on the back seat.

The East London roads were jam-packed with traffic and Tom could only edge the car slowly along rain-soaked streets, which was making the journey much longer than usual.

Lucy had wrapped a comforting arm around her little sister, who snuggled closer as the windscreen wipers swept to and fro and the rain pounded on the roof of the car.

Outside, pedestrians hurried in different directions trying to escape the heavy rain, but Lucy didn't notice them. Her thoughts were fixed on what had happened at the pool. The scene replayed over and over in her mind. It had been so horrible. And seeing Sarah Hammond standing there with tears in her eyes was just… Actually, Lucy didn't know how it had made her feel. Sad? Confused? Upset for everyone, including Sarah Hammond?

She thought back to the moment their eyes had met and was suddenly shocked to realise that it hadn't been like seeing a complete stranger. There had been something between them. Lucy didn't know what it was – she couldn't explain it to herself or anyone else – but in that instant there had been … *something*.

Lucy was completely lost in her thoughts when she felt a light tap on one knee and turned to see Rose looking anxiously at her.

'Are you all right?' Rose whispered.

Lucy smiled and nodded. Usually she was the one asking if her friend was all right, but for once, they had swapped roles and Rose looked genuinely worried.

They had said very little about the row as they got dressed afterwards in the changing rooms. Lucy was too upset to talk much, but she knew that Rose would want to know exactly what was going on and decided that she would tell her later, when she felt better. Because right then, Lucy felt bewildered and miserable.

It was hot inside the car and the windows were beginning to steam up with condensation. Lucy wiped clear the glass next to her, wishing that she could make her own thoughts as clear this easily.

She stared out into the wet, bustling street and sighed. Maybe Rose could help her make sense of the total confusion she was feeling.

Eleven

Weeks often just flew by for Lucy. One day was very much like the next – she trained, she went to school and she trained again. Nothing out of the ordinary happened to disturb her routine. Before she knew it, the days had flown by and Sunday's rest day had arrived. And then she started all over again.

But this week was different. To Lucy, it seemed an age since the telephone call from Sarah Hammond had disturbed the peace of last Sunday evening. But it was just one week. In seven days, Lucy's whole world had been turned upside down.

This Sunday, she was reading the sports supplement of the newspaper but finding it hard to concentrate. Her mum was flicking through a magazine and seemed equally listless.

'Are you okay, Mum?' Lucy asked, putting down the paper.

Jo glanced up from the magazine and shrugged her shoulders. 'I've had better weeks. We all have.'

'That's just what I was thinking,' Lucy answered. 'Why did this have to happen? Why did she have to turn up now?'

'I don't know,' Jo said, with a shake of her head. 'But we can't let things go on like this. We have to do something, one way or another. You know how tense it all was last night; no one speaking, not even Mia. I'm glad she's gone to play at her friend's house this morning.'

Lucy nodded. 'I've never seen Dad so upset.'

At that moment the door opened and Tom came in. His face had lost its usual sunny appearance and he looked tired and drawn. He glanced from Jo to Lucy and then back again. 'I can guess what you two have been talking about,' he said.

Jo raised her eyebrows. 'There isn't much else on any of our minds right now, is there?'

'You're right,' Tom replied, sitting down in an armchair. 'But I've made a decision.'

Lucy looked anxiously at Jo, wondering what Tom's decision might mean for them all.

'Go on, then,' Jo said.

'I've decided that I don't want you to go to the pool for the next few days,' Tom said to Lucy.

'What? But why?' Lucy was shocked. Surely her dad didn't mean this. She couldn't afford to miss any training sessions.

'Because that ... that *woman* might be there.'

'Tom,' said Jo, 'can you please stop calling her "that woman". She's Sarah. Let's just use her name from now on.'

Tom looked as though it would hurt him to mention the name. He sighed. 'All right, *Sarah* might be there. She's been once and she's probably been there before. So she's likely to turn up again at any time.'

'Dad, I've got the most important race of the season coming up next Saturday. I've got to train.'

'I know that, but it's not the only pool in London. If we speak to Dave, he'll understand. I've thought it through. It'll mean a bit more travelling time, but we can do it. I just don't want ... *Sarah* ruining everything for you, Lucy. Not when you're so close to making the team for the Games.'

Jo shook her head. 'Tom, we can't run away from Sarah like this. Changing swimming pools isn't the answer.'

'Then what *is* the answer? I don't want her in our lives.'

'But it's not up to you, Tom,' said Jo. 'It's Lucy's decision.' She turned to Lucy. 'I've been wondering if it would be best if you did meet her, just once. And then you can decide about seeing her more in the future. If that's what you want.'

Lucy had slept badly the previous night, wondering

whether or not she should meet Sarah, turning the question over and over in her mind. Since the scene at the swimming pool she felt a deep curiosity about her natural mother and part of her wanted to do exactly as Jo suggested.

But Lucy had dedicated most of the past four years to the ultimate goal of making the British Paralympic team for the London 2012 Games. Success was now so close – almost within touching distance – and a win or even a second-place finish in the Paralympic Trials the following Saturday would do so much to influence the team selectors. It might even make up their minds.

Lucy had thought all this through for what seemed like for ever before finally falling into a troubled sleep. And she only slept because she had finally come to a decision, which was that she couldn't and wouldn't let anything affect her preparations for the race.

'No,' Lucy said. 'I don't want to meet her. Not before next Saturday, anyway. It's my most important race – not just of the season, but maybe of my racing career so far.'

Tom smiled. 'So you're okay with training somewhere else this week?'

Lucy nodded. 'Yes – if you really think it will help and if Dave agrees.'

'Oh, Dave will agree,' Tom said. 'He wants what's best for you. Like I do. Like we all do.' He looked at Jo. 'Eh, love?'

Jo didn't look quite so convinced. 'I suppose so,' she said, with a shrug of her shoulders.

Later that afternoon, Lucy had a long conversation on her mobile with Rose. Her friend had known for years that Jo was Lucy's step-mum. It was no secret; most people knew or found out once they had been friends with Lucy for a while. But even though she had seen Sarah briefly at the pool the previous day, the full story of Sarah Hammond's return to Lucy's life came as a surprise to Rose.

'So I've agreed that I won't train at our pool this week,' Lucy finished. 'That way, I won't risk bumping into Sarah Hammond.'

'I'll miss you,' Rose said. 'But are you really sure that you don't want to meet … Sarah?' It seemed that even Rose found it a little difficult to mention the name. 'I think I would, if I were in your situation.'

'I am sure,' Lucy replied. 'At least, I'm sure that I don't want to meet her this week, before my race on Saturday. After that, who knows? I may feel differently. But for now, I want to put Sarah Hammond from my mind completely.'

'Does anyone else know about this?'

'Dad's spoken to Dave about it, so it's just you two who know the whole story. I don't want everyone to know what's happening – that's why I'm telling you on the phone and not at school tomorrow. You will keep it to yourself, won't you?'

'Of course I will,' Rose answered.

'I don't want any fuss or any more upset this week.'

'I understand, Lucy,' said Rose. 'It's such an important week for you. And I'll help you all I can.'

'Promise?' Lucy asked.

'I promise,' Rose said.

Twelve

Lucy wasn't the only person to have made an important decision. Sarah Hammond had also spent a restless night before finally making up her mind over the problem that had kept her awake for so long.

As Lucy sat in her bedroom in Newham that Sunday afternoon, speaking to Rose on the phone, Sarah was on the other side of London, walking by the River Thames with her friend Jill.

'I know that it was wrong of me to try to see Lucy that way,' Sarah said as they walked. 'I should have been patient like you suggested.'

'It couldn't have been easy for you wondering all the time if Lucy would call,' Jill said.

They came to a wooden bench overlooking the river and sat down, gazing out at the dark water. The river was high after the recent heavy rain and water flowed swiftly towards the sea.

'I was offered another cruise last week,' Sarah said. 'This morning I decided to take it, so I sent an email to the office accepting the offer.'

Jill looked surprised. 'When do you leave?'

'Next Sunday. We sail from Southampton for the Caribbean.'

Jill nodded slowly. It was a few moments before she replied. 'You don't think you're being a little hasty? It's almost as though you're...' She stopped.

Sarah smiled. 'Were you going to say that I'm running away again?'

'It's your decision, Sarah,' Jill said.

Seagulls wheeled overhead, gliding effortlessly on the breeze and then diving down to scoop up scraps floating on the water.

'I've caused so much hurt by rushing in instead of waiting,' Sarah said sadly. 'I saw how I'd upset Tom and his wife and their other little daughter. And Lucy, of course. I've upset Lucy most of all and I'm *so* sorry. The best thing I can do for everyone concerned is to go away.'

'Everyone concerned?' Jill asked. 'Does that include you?'

Sarah didn't reply.

'How long will you be gone?'

'A couple of months – maybe longer. I'll pick up another ship when we reach our destination and sail somewhere else.'

'So does this mean you're giving up on your

daughter...?' Jill asked. 'It may not be what she wants.'

Sarah stared up at the cawing seagulls as they sailed and swooped in the blustery sky. 'I'm not giving up. I've written Lucy a letter, telling her that I'm going away on Sunday. I've said that I realise I was wrong to try to come back into her life after all this time and that I'm glad to see that she's happy. And I am glad, Jill. I really am.'

'I know you are,' Jill answered softly.

'But I've also said that if ever Lucy wants to, she can contact me at home. And I've told her that I'll leave it to her to decide what happens from now on.'

Jill shrugged. 'Perhaps writing is a good idea,' she said uncertainly.

'I hope so,' said Sarah. 'I've made so many mistakes in the past – I don't want to make even more.' The sharp wind came cutting in from across the river, making her shiver. 'Shall we get going?' she asked.

Jill nodded and they got up and strode quickly along the footpath.

'So have you posted the letter?' Jill asked as they walked.

'I wrote it this morning,' Sarah said. 'I thought I'd leave it until I get back and then read it through again to make sure that I've got it exactly right. Then I'll post it tonight.'

Low, dark clouds were gathering across the river

and the wind had become even colder.

'I think we should turn back,' Jill said. 'It looks like there could be more rain.'

As they turned to retrace their steps, Sarah's mobile phone began to ring. She took it from her pocket and looked at the screen.

'It's Tom's number,' she said, as the phone continued to ring. 'Do you think Lucy's trying to call me?'

Jill smiled. 'There's only one way to find out.'

Sarah pressed the button to accept the call and put the phone to her ear. 'Hello?'

'It's Tom,' a deep voice said coldly.

'Oh, hello Tom.'

'I'm just calling to let you know that there's no point in turning up at the swimming pool this week because Lucy won't be there. She doesn't want to see you and I don't want you upsetting her and the rest of my family any more.'

Sarah's heart sank. 'I promise you, Tom, that I didn't mean to upset anyone and—'

'You never mean to upset anyone, Sarah,' Tom interrupted. 'But you're very good at doing it. Now, I've told you: Lucy doesn't doesn't want to see you and I don't want you making contact with her again. So please stay away. Goodbye.'

Before Sarah had a chance to say another word, the line went dead. For a moment she thought of calling

Tom back, but then she sighed and returned the phone to her pocket.

'It was Tom,' she explained. Sadly, she told her friend what he'd said.

They walked on slowly as the first spots of rain began to fall.

'Does this mean that you won't send the letter after all?' Jill asked.

Sarah stopped walking and turned to look at her friend. 'I really want Lucy to know how I feel,' she said, ignoring the raindrops. 'What I also told her in the letter was that I promise if ever she needs me, I'll be there for her. I want her to know that, Jill, because I mean it. I'll *never* break that promise. Never.'

'But what about what Tom? What if he sees the letter? He'll be furious.'

'He won't see it,' Sarah said. 'This is between Lucy and me. I don't want to cause any more upset for her or her family, so I'm not going to send the letter. But I'm going to make absolutely sure Lucy gets it.'

Thirteen

Training at a different pool felt strange for Lucy. She was swimming alone, with none of her teammates around to work with. Most of all, she missed the banter. It was always an important part of the session. After the hard work came the chatter and jokes, the discussions about form and targets for the rest of the season and beyond. But today was different and Lucy was finding it a little lonely.

There was no swimming club based at the new pool, so Dave had made a special arrangement with the manager to have a lane marked off for Lucy.

As she ploughed up and down under the watchful eyes of her trainer, she worked on picking up the pace in the second half of a race. But it wasn't going as well as Dave or Lucy had hoped.

'You're looking a little sluggish,' Dave called as Lucy made a turn to start another length.

Lucy *felt* a little sluggish. Like all racing swimmers, she could tell if the water in a pool was fast or slow. It was one of those things that she couldn't really explain. How could water be fast or slow? But somehow it could, and this pool was slow. It wasn't designed for racing and that seemed to make a difference.

Dave followed Lucy along the poolside and watched her turn for the last time.

'Come on, let's have a really strong final length!' he called. 'Go for it.'

Lucy did her very best, digging deep to find extra speed. When she was battling like this, she always thought back to an article she had once read by a former British Olympic champion, Judy Grinham…

Even when you think you can't go faster, you can. You have got it inside you, use it. That's what happened to me in the Olympic Games final and that's why I won.

The inspirational words came to Lucy again as she surged down the final length.

'Much better,' Dave called. 'Much, much better. You suddenly look like a swimmer again.'

As Lucy touched the wall, Dave clicked the stopwatch he was holding. He checked the time and shrugged. 'You're not going to break any world records, but it wasn't bad, and that last length was terrific. What happened?'

Lucy grinned. 'Someone spoke to me and told me to go faster. And it wasn't you.'

Dave glanced around the pool and laughed. It was very quiet, with just a few fun swimmers splashing about on the far side. 'Oh, really? And who might that have been?' Dave asked.

'That's my secret.' Lucy smiled. 'But she often speaks to me.'

'Well, good for her,' Dave said. 'You'd better make sure that she has a word with you at the trials on Saturday. It's going to be tough. You'll be racing against all the top girls in the country.'

Lucy was suddenly very serious. 'I know that, Dave, and I'll be ready.'

Jo collected Lucy after training and on the way home they drove close to the Olympic Park.

After the rain of the previous two days, the weather had cleared and the whole area – with its parkland walks, shimmering waterways and giant arenas – was bathed in late sunshine.

The towering Olympic Stadium dominated the site, but as always, Lucy's eyes went to the Aquatics Centre, which was now fitted with the additional banks of seating required for the Games. When the competitions were over, the extra seating – sprouting like wings from the main building – would be taken down and the Centre would once again reveal its true beauty to the world.

Jo smiled as she saw Lucy gazing at the Centre. 'You'll be swimming there in the Paralympic Games, I know it. And we'll all be there cheering you on.'

'I hope so, Mum,' Lucy said. Her eyes shifted to the Olympic Village buildings. During the competitions, these would be home to the athletes from every nation. 'And maybe I'll be living there for a couple of weeks.' She turned and smiled at Jo. 'I've read that the Village is lovely – really nice apartments. But even if I do get to stay there for the Games, it won't be like home. Nothing could ever be like being at home with you and Dad and Mia.'

Jo realised that Lucy's words were partly meant to reassure her after the upset and worries of the previous week. And they did make her feel better. But the words also reminded Jo that Sarah Hammond was still very much on Lucy's mind. 'Are you sure that you're okay about not seeing Sarah?' she asked gently. 'I wouldn't mind. And you know that we could talk your dad round if we had to – we always can if we try hard enough.'

Lucy laughed. 'I'm sure,' she said. 'For now, anyway. And even if I do see Sarah in the future, nothing will ever change the way I feel about you. You're my mum and you're the best mum in the world.'

They were almost home and Jo smiled happily as she turned the car into their road and began looking for a parking space.

A vehicle pulled away from the kerbside just in front of them and Jo carefully edged their car into the vacant space. She switched off the engine and turned to Lucy. 'So, let's go in and see if the best *dad* in the world has cheered up a little, shall we?'

Fourteen

Rose went to the pool as usual for Tuesday's club night. She loved being part of the club and training with the other swimmers. She even liked to race, although she very rarely won or even finished in the top three. But it didn't worry her because, for Rose, swimming was mainly for fun.

This week was different. Rose's best friend wasn't at the pool – she was training elsewhere. And Rose missed Lucy, exactly as she'd told her she would.

But, without Lucy to chat to and watch as she trained, Rose found herself working harder than she normally would. She was surprised to find that she actually enjoyed it more.

Rose's best and favourite stroke was the backstroke. She was a very elegant backstroke swimmer, with long arms and lovely technique. Everyone said that she looked fantastic as she swam. That was the good part. The not-so-good part was that she usually didn't go very fast.

But this time she surged up and down the pool like a champion, earning admiring looks and encouraging words from other swimmers and the club coach. As Rose swam, she found herself wishing that Lucy were there to see her and hear the compliments she was receiving. At the end of the session, she climbed, panting, from the pool. She stood at the side and laughed out loud.

'What's so funny?' another girl asked.

Rose was breathing deeply. 'Me!' she gasped. 'I never realised that hard work could be quite so much fun. It was totally cool.'

She tottered off to the changing room, still chuckling. Her dad was due to pick her up and Rose knew that he was almost always late. There was no need to hurry.

'I'll wash my hair and have a nice, long, hot shower,' she told herself as she opened her locker. 'After all that hard work, I deserve it.'

Sarah was anxiously pacing up and down the reception area, wondering what could have happened to Lucy's friend. She couldn't possibly have left the leisure centre without Sarah spotting her.

Lots of swimmers, young and old, had left the building, but there was no sign of the girl she was looking for. Sarah had the letter for Lucy in her pocket and she planned to ask her daughter's friend to pass it on. They were obviously close. Sarah had watched them swimming and playing together in the pool the previous Saturday.

This evening, Sarah had sat in the gallery again, knowing that Lucy wouldn't be in the pool, but hoping that her friend would be. And she was. Sarah watched the entire session, waiting for the girl to leave the pool to get changed. Once she did, Sarah moved down to the reception area to wait for her to leave the building.

But she was still waiting.

There was nothing in the letter that Tom shouldn't know, but Sarah felt certain that he would be angry if he knew that she had written to their daughter.

And Sarah didn't think that was fair, because she desperately wanted Lucy to know that she would always be there for her, if ever she needed her and whenever that might be. Sarah wanted her daughter to know that she would never let her down again.

Deep in her heart, Sarah hoped that when Lucy read the letter and learned that her mother was leaving on a long cruise the following Sunday, she might make contact and they would meet, however briefly.

But that was only a faint hope. The most important thing

for Sarah was for Lucy to know how she felt about her.

Sarah sighed. More and more people were leaving the building. Surely Lucy's friend couldn't *still* be changing?

And then the doors leading to the female changing room swung open and the girl finally emerged. She was looking down, fiddling with the earphones of an iPod and didn't spot Sarah as she approached.

'Excuse me?'

The girl stopped, raised her head and stared when she saw Sarah.

'My name is Sarah Hammond,' she said. 'I'm Lucy's m—'

'I know who you are,' Rose interrupted. 'I saw you on Saturday.'

'Oh. Oh, yes. Look, I'm sorry you saw that. I'm sorry anyone had to see it, especially Lucy.'

'Lucy isn't here.'

'I know.' Sarah nodded. 'It's you I wanted to see.'

Rose's eyes widened. 'Me? Why do you want to see *me*?'

Sarah dug a hand into her jacket pocket and pulled out the envelope containing the letter. 'I was hoping that you would give this to Lucy. Will you, please? She held out the letter, waiting for Rose to take it.

Rose didn't move. 'I'm not sure. I don't know if I should.'

Only moments earlier, as she'd left the changing room, Rose had been feeling fantastic and ready to tell her dad all about her brilliant training session. Now though, she felt unsure and uneasy.

And Sarah could see the uncertainty in Rose's eyes. 'I'm sorry,' she said gently, trying to look and sound as reassuring as she could. 'I don't know your name.'

'It's Rose.'

Sarah nodded and smiled. 'Rose, I know you're a good friend of Lucy's. I could see that on Saturday.'

'She's my best friend, and I'm hers.'

'So you probably know about me and what happened when Lucy was a baby?'

Rose nodded but said nothing.

Sarah glanced down at the letter. 'I've tried very hard to explain some things to Lucy in this letter, about the past and the future. It's very, very important to me that she reads it. Will you give it to her for me?' She held out the letter again. 'Please?'

Through the large windows at the front of the building, Rose spotted a large four-by-four vehicle swing into the car park. 'That's my dad,' she said to Sarah. 'I have to go now.' But Rose didn't move and Sarah edged a little closer.

'Please?' Sarah repeated, glancing down at the envelope.

Rose's eyes moved quickly from Sarah to the envelope and back to Sarah again. Then, without a word, she quickly snatched the envelope from Sarah's hand and hurried away towards the car park.

'Enjoy the swim?' Rose's dad asked as his daughter fastened her seat belt.

'It was great, thanks,' Rose replied.

'Good,' her dad said, quickly driving away from the car park. 'Was Lucy there?'

'I told you this morning, Dad. Lucy's not training at the pool this week.'

'Did you?' Her dad obviously didn't remember their conversation. 'Why's that, then?

Rose sighed. 'It doesn't matter.'

'You two haven't fallen out again, have you?'

'*No!*'

Rose's dad glanced over at her, as if surprised at the irritation in her voice. 'I only asked, Rose, that's all. There's no need to be grumpy with me.'

'Sorry, Dad,' Rose said. 'I was thinking about … swimming.'

But Rose wasn't thinking about swimming. She was

actually thinking about the letter she had crammed into one of her pockets. It seemed as though it was almost burning a hole through the material, desperate to be opened and read – by Lucy.

And that was why Rose was feeling so confused and concerned. It was the look of desperation in Sarah's eyes that had finally convinced her to take the letter. But now that Rose had the letter, she had no idea what she was going to do with it.

Just two days before, Lucy had told her very clearly that she didn't want to think about Sarah Hammond during the vitally important week building up to her big races on Saturday.

This meant that Lucy wouldn't want to read the letter.

But Sarah had told Rose that it was very important that Lucy *did* read the letter.

And then there was Rose's promise to help Lucy all she could. Rose would never break a promise. She finally made up her mind about what she was going to do.

'Sunday,' she said quietly to herself.

'What?' her dad said. 'What about Sunday?'

'Oh, nothing,' Rose said. 'I was just thinking aloud.'

Rose had made her decision. She was going to give Lucy the letter on Sunday, when the big races were over.

Fifteen

Dave eased down on Lucy's training in the days leading up to Saturday. He wanted her strong, fresh and race-fit for the vital event.

The build-up had gone well. Lucy had got used to working in the other pool and was feeling ready for the two events that would go a long way to deciding whether or not she made the Paralympic team for London 2012.

Lucy had achieved the qualifying times in her two strongest events, the 200m and 400m. The trials meeting brought together all the swimmers who had achieved the qualifying times; they'd now compete head to head. The selectors would still have the final say, but a win or top-two finish today would virtually seal a place in the team.

Lucy felt good as she made her way along the poolside with the other girls taking part in the 200m race. It was going to be tough, but just as Lucy had told Dave, she was ready for it.

The event was being held in Manchester, at the top-ranking pool once used for the Commonwealth Games. Lucy had swum there many times before and always enjoyed the experience. The pool had fast water – exactly what swimmers wanted.

The girls reached the starting end and waited to be introduced to the crowd packed into the spectators' galleries.

Lucy gazed upwards, trying to pick out her family and Rose, who had travelled up in the car with them. She knew that they were all there, but Lucy couldn't see them. For a moment, she wondered if Sarah Hammond might also be in the crowd, but she quickly pushed the thought away. She had to focus on the race. Nothing could be allowed to disturb her concentration.

The starter began to announce the names and one by one the girls got onto the starting blocks and waved to the crowd, each receiving loud cheers and applause.

Lucy's name was called and as she stepped up she heard enormous cheering from one area of the gallery. Looking up, she spotted her family and Rose. She smiled and waved at them.

She felt tense, but ready to swim and to race.

The starter told the girls to get to their marks and the crowd fell completely silent.

Lucy crouched, toes curled over the edge of the

block, body leaning forward and poised to dive.

Then the starting pistol sounded and the eight girls hurled themselves towards the waiting water.

Sarah had finished her packing. She sat drinking a cup of coffee, staring at the two large suitcases that would accompany her on the journey to Southampton.

Every so often she glanced towards her phone, willing it to ring. Once or twice, she even checked to make sure that the line wasn't dead. But even though the phone was working perfectly, no calls came through.

All week Sarah had clung on to the slight hope that after reading the letter, Lucy might call to speak to her before she left on the cruise. But Sarah had no idea that Lucy hadn't seen the letter; she didn't even know of its existence. Rose still had the letter and had stuck to her decision not to give it to her friend until after her big day.

Sarah sighed, finished her coffee and went to the sink to wash up the cup and saucer. She stood, gazing out through the window, thinking over the life she had led since the end of her marriage to Tom.

It had been lonely at times. Sarah had worked as a

teacher for a number of years, and then decided she wanted to travel and became a swimming instructor on cruise ships. Sarah enjoyed the job; it meant that she got to see many exciting places around the world, but she knew that there was always something missing in her life – her daughter. But sadly for her, it seemed that Lucy didn't want to know her. And Sarah couldn't blame her daughter for feeling that way after fourteen years of no contact at all.

She wiped the cup and saucer dry and put them away in a cupboard. Then she turned to take a last look at her flat. It would be at least two months before she saw it again, perhaps longer.

Sarah took out her photo of Lucy as a baby.

'Where are you?' Sarah said softly as she stared at the photo. 'And what are you doing right now?'

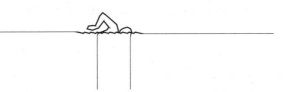

'Lu-cy! Lu-cy! Lu-cy! Lu-cy! Lu-cy!' Rose and Mia chanted together, clapping their hands in rhythm with the word. 'Lu-cy! Lu-cy!'

Lucy was battling up the final length in the 200m race. It was so close between the three girls leading the race – and Lucy was one of them.

The crowd shouted and roared encouragement to all the swimmers, so loudly that it sounded as though the roof might lift right off the building.

'Lu-cy! Lu-cy! Lu-cy!' screamed Rose and Mia.

'She's going to do it!' Jo yelled to Tom above the noise of the cheering.

'It's so close!' Tom yelled back. 'So, so close!'

The swimmers reached the final ten metres, heads down, arms turning, feet kicking.

Five more metres ... they were almost within touching distance.

'Lu-cy!'

One metre ... and then they touched the wall. It was all over. The girls turned to look at the giant electronic board that would show their times and their finishing places.

The swimmer in the lane next to Lucy suddenly shouted, 'Yes!'

Quickly, Lucy and the others checked their own times and positions.

Lucy had finished second, just a fraction behind the winner. It was a terrific result – and Lucy's fastest time of the season – but she felt a twinge of disappointment as she leaned on the lane divider and smiled at the winner.

'Well done,' she said. 'Great race.'

Sarah sat back in her seat and watched London gradually slip away as the train for Southampton wound its way from the city and out through the suburbs.

For a while, the train ran close to the River Thames and Sarah caught glimpses of the London Eye, Big Ben and the Houses of Parliament. Then huge buildings and landmarks gave way to row after row of old redbrick houses and bustling streets.

The train stopped a couple of times and more passengers piled on, but soon the suburbs were left behind and the city gave way to countryside.

The sun shone on fields and meadows. It was a beautiful day, but Sarah's heart was heavy.

Tomorrow she would set sail on another exciting adventure, but right now she felt that she would give anything for just a few brief words with her daughter.

The train pulled into another station and more passengers got on. The carriage was almost full now. There were just two empty seats, directly opposite Sarah. A woman of about her age and a teenage girl, probably similar in age to Lucy, took the seats and started to chat.

From their conversation, Sarah quickly overheard that they were mother and daughter and that they had spent a happy day out together and were now on their way home.

Sarah turned away and stared out of the window, trying to block out their conversation and thinking of the days that she had never spent with Lucy.

'Please call,' she whispered.

This time, Lucy told herself, she was not going to be beaten. The 400m was her strongest event and even though she had battled through an exhausting race earlier in the day she was determined that no one would defeat her again.

The cheers ringing around the pool were as loud as any during the entire event. There had been a succession of incredibly close races, record-breaking times and outstanding performances.

And this race, with a little more than a length to go, was building towards another fantastic finale.

Lucy was one of a group of four swimmers who had moved clear of the other girls, but as in the 200m, there was nothing between the leaders.

Almost as one, they turned and kicked away from the wall to begin the final length.

'Lu-cy! Lu-cy! Lu-cy! Lu-cy!' Rose and Mia chanted.

Lucy couldn't hear them above the noise of the crowd. All she could hear were the inspirational words of her idol, Judy Grinham: *Even when you think you can't go faster, you can. You have got it inside you, use it.*

Lucy was smiling inside as she swam. She could go faster. She would go faster. And she did go faster.

There were gasps of amazement from the crowd as, within ten metres, Lucy had surged clear of the other swimmers.

'Wow!' shouted Dave from his place in the crowd. 'Go girl, go!'

'She's got it this time!' yelled Tom. 'She's got it!'

'Lu-cy! Lu-cy! Lu-cy! Lu-cy!'

'Come on, Lucy!' shouted Jo, with tears in her eyes.

Lucy moved further and further ahead. And with twenty metres remaining there was clear water between her and the girl in second place.

No one could get near Lucy. She increased her lead with every stroke and won by more than five metres. She even had time to turn and look back to see the other girls finish.

The electronic board showed that she had shattered her personal best and posted a time that put her up with the best recorded anywhere in the world that year.

The pool rang with cheers and applause as Lucy raised her arms in triumph and thought of London 2012.

Sixteen

It was a long drive home from Manchester. Mia, worn out from the excitement of the day, had fallen asleep even before the vehicle was out of the city.

Tom and Jo chatted excitedly for a while, filled with pride at their daughter's success, while Lucy and Rose sat quietly in the back, exchanging a few soft words over the head of the sleeping Mia. Once they made it back to London, Rose was going to be staying over for the night, so there would be plenty of time to talk later.

By the time they reached the motorway, a comfortable silence had settled on the car's occupants.

Tom switched on the radio and as she listened to the music, Lucy soon found herself thinking through her races again, reliving them stroke by stroke.

It had been an amazing day and Lucy felt sure that she was a huge step closer to the ParalympicsGB team. But with the races over, there was time now to think of other things, and Lucy's mind quickly turned to Sarah.

Many times during the week, Lucy had thought of her natural mother, but each time she had pushed the thoughts away, telling herself that she must focus totally on the races to come. But this time she did nothing to stop herself wondering about Sarah. And she felt her heart beating faster as finally she admitted to herself for the very first time that she *did* want to meet Sarah.

There was no doubt any more and Lucy smiled as she realised that now she wasn't thinking of Sarah as Sarah Hammond. Now it was just Sarah. And that, Lucy decided, sounded much better.

But how would she contact Sarah? It wouldn't be easy, Lucy thought, as she noticed that as well as a thudding heart, she now also seemed to have huge butterflies fluttering inside her chest. She would have to talk her dad round to the idea, and that would take time. But that wasn't a problem; there was plenty of time.

Lucy settled back in her seat and closed her eyes, exhausted but happy. She was too excited to sleep, but it was nice just to sit back and let the music from the car radio wash over her.

As the car ate up the miles and London came closer, Lucy wondered if anyone else in the vehicle had thought about Sarah since the journey had begun. Her dad, maybe? Or Jo?

At home, Sarah's name had remained unspoken all

week, but now that the big races were over, Lucy knew that it wouldn't stay that way. It couldn't. Sarah was somehow there with them, hidden from sight, but there as if waiting to be brought into the open again. Lucy felt the butterflies in her chest take flight again as she told herself that if no one else mentioned Sarah very soon, then she most definitely would.

The song playing on the radio came to an end and Lucy opened her eyes and glanced over at Rose, who also looked deep in thought.

Lucy would have been amazed to learn that Rose was also thinking about Sarah – and the letter she had in her back pocket. She'd have been even more amazed if she'd known what her mother had written on the pages of that letter.

All that information was so close at hand, but it might just as well have been a million miles away.

Lucy tapped her friend on the leg and when Rose turned her head and looked at her, she asked, 'You okay?'

Rose nodded. 'Just thinking.'

'What about?

'Nothing really. Tell you tomorrow.'

Tom had put up a camp bed in Lucy's bedroom and the girls were changing into pyjamas. They were both weary and red-eyed; it had been a very long and exciting day.

Rose was about to drape her jeans over a chair when the envelope, folded in the centre, slipped from her back pocket and dropped onto the carpet.

Lucy saw the envelope fall. As it landed, the envelope slowly unfolded like a butterfly's wings, and she saw her name written across the centre in blue ink.

She looked at Rose. 'Why've you got an envelope with my name on it?'

'Er ... er...' Rose stammered. 'I was going to give it to you tomorrow.' Out of the water, Rose usually moved more quickly than her friend. But she was surprised when she went to pick up the envelope and found that Lucy had beaten her to it.

'But this isn't your writing,' Lucy said.

'No, it isn't.'

Lucy looked at her friend, waiting for her to continue.

'Rose?'

'I'll tell you about it tomorrow, shall I?' Rose yawned, trying in vain to shift Lucy's attention from the envelope. 'After we've had a good night's sleep.'

But Lucy wasn't going to be put off. 'Why tomorrow? Why can't you tell me about it now?'

'I can't. Not really.'

'Why can't you?

'I promised that I wouldn't.'

'Promised who?'

'Myself.'

Lucy sat on the bed and stared at the envelope in her hands. 'Rose, whose writing is this?'

Rose hesitated for a moment and then the words came tumbling out. 'I didn't want to tell you about it until tomorrow. It's not a secret – the letter, I mean. I've had it for days and it's for you. But I didn't want you to be upset and I promised I'd help you, didn't I? So that's why I didn't give you the letter. And you weren't upset and you swam better than I've ever seen you swim, so I did the right thing. Didn't I? Please tell me that I did the right thing, Lucy.'

Lucy looked completely confused. 'Rose, what are you talking about?'

Rose sighed, sat on the bed next to her friend and nodded slowly towards the envelope. 'It's from Sarah Hammond.'

'From Sarah!' Lucy gasped, much louder than she intended.

'Shhh!' Rose said. 'Your parents will hear us.'

'Buy why have you got it?' Lucy said in a loud whisper.

'Because she gave it to me.'

'But why? When?'

Quickly, quietly and as simply as she could, Rose explained how she had met Lucy's mother when she was leaving the pool and how Sarah had given her the letter.

'But then I didn't know what to do,' Rose said as Lucy listened, wide-eyed. 'You said that you wanted to put Sarah out of your mind and that you didn't want any more upset this week, so I thought it would be best to give it to you tomorrow. I was right, wasn't I?'

Lucy's thoughts were racing, but she smiled to reassure her anxious friend. 'Of course you were right. It was really thoughtful of you. And it must have been hard for you, keeping this to yourself all week.'

Rose sighed. 'You have no idea how hard it was.'

The two girls sat side by side on the bed, staring at the slightly crumpled envelope Lucy held in her hands.

'Are you going to open it now?' Rose asked.

'I'm a bit scared of what the letter will say,' Lucy answered.

'Maybe it would be best to leave it until the morning, then.'

Lucy shook her head. 'No, I've got to know what Sarah's written to me.' Slowly and nervously, she tore open the sealed envelope.

Seventeen

Lights sparkled and glistened on the calm surface of Southampton Water. Huge, ocean-going cruise ships, towering up from the quayside, sat peacefully at rest.

Far across the strait of the Solent, the dark shadowy outline of the Isle of Wight, dotted with tiny specks of light, could just be glimpsed.

Much nearer, a few small boats moved almost noiselessly through the cold, black water, tumbling white waves breaking from their bows as they searched out a safe berth for the night.

There was little sound, just the occasional slap of water against the side of a ship, the echoing hoot of a tugboat or the haunting screech of a gull, swooping like a phantom out of the darkness.

Sarah was on board the ship that was to carry her far across the ocean the following day. It was late, but Sarah couldn't sleep. Her mind was racing and the small cabin she was sharing with another member of the crew had suddenly seemed much too tiny. So she had walked round and round the open decks, trying and failing to calm herself. Now she leaned on the rail, four decks above the water, gazing out at the tranquil late-night scene and feeling that she would never be able to rest until she heard something, anything, from her daughter.

Tomorrow, when the passengers came on board, the ship would almost instantly change from the peaceful, floating island it was now into a bustling, busy town, full of shops, restaurants and any number of leisure and sporting clubs.

And people. There would be hundreds of people, many of them demanding Sarah's attention and care. She would be frantically busy before the ship had even left the harbour.

Perhaps, she thought, as she stared across the water, it would be better then. Easier. Being busy would take her mind off Lucy.

'Perhaps,' she said softly. 'But I doubt it.'

She turned away from the rail and set off on one more walk around the deck.

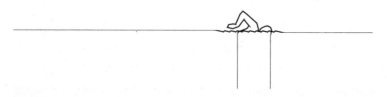

Lucy's eyes were moist with tears. She had read the letter through quickly. Then she read it again, slowly, pausing after almost every paragraph to think over what Sarah had written, about the past, the present and the future.

As she learned how the separation between them had hurt her mother over the years, the words had touched Lucy deeply. She clasped the sheets of writing paper tightly in one hand and wiped away the tears with the other.

'She's leaving,' she said quietly to Rose. 'Tomorrow.'

'What?' asked Rose. 'Where's she going?'

Lucy gave the letter to her friend. 'You can read it.'

'Are you sure?'

Lucy nodded. 'I want you to know what she's said.'

Rose read the letter, looking up at Lucy from time to time, her face revealing her feelings. 'I should have given this to you earlier,' she said, as soon as she reached the end. 'But I didn't know about the job or the cruise. She didn't tell me. How could I have known that she was going away?'

'It's not your fault, Rose,' said Lucy. 'You did exactly as I asked. But I have to see her before she leaves.'

'See her?' said Rose. 'But how can you? She's in Southampton. And your dad would never allow you to go there. He doesn't want you to see her at all.'

'I know, but I have to go,' Lucy said, determinedly. 'If I don't, she'll think that I don't care. And I do care, very much.'

'Can't you … can't you just call her and speak to her on the phone?'

'There's no mobile number in the letter.'

'Why didn't she give you her mobile number?'

'Well, she probably didn't think that you'd hold onto the letter for nearly a week.'

Rose looked as though she was about to burst into tears. 'Oh, Lucy…'

'It's all right,' Lucy said quickly. 'I know why you did it.' She glanced at the letter again. 'Sarah put her home number and her address. She must have thought I'd call her there.'

'But she could still have left you a mobile number. Why didn't she?'

'I don't know,' Lucy said irritably. Then she was struck by a thought. 'Because they probably don't work out at sea, that's why. And anyway, speaking on the phone wouldn't be the same. I have to see her, even if it's just for a little while.'

'But there isn't time to get all the way to Southampton tomorrow, is there?' Rose asked. She thought for a moment. 'Where is Southampton?'

'On the south coast,' Lucy said. 'And there's plenty of time to get there. I'm going to see her.'

Rose sighed and then nodded. 'Then I'm coming with you.'

Eighteen

Lucy and Rose made their plans long into the night.

Tom tapped gently on the bedroom door and called, 'It's late, girls. Time for lights out!' But as soon as he'd gone, they continued with their scheme to get to Southampton so that Lucy could meet Sarah before the ship sailed.

They had Sarah's home address and phone number, but neither were any help now that she was already in Southampton. But in the letter Sarah had also mentioned the name of the ship she would be sailing on the following afternoon.

By the light of Lucy's laptop, the girls went online and found the ship and the cruise company, along with details of the cruise and the time of departure from Southampton.

'Look at all those amazing places the ship's going to,' Rose whispered as they gazed at the laptop screen. 'It sounds really cool. Maybe we could go, too.'

Lucy smiled. 'Maybe another time. Right now, we

just have to make sure that I get to see Sarah.'

'But even if we reach Southampton on time, how can we let Sarah know that you'll be there?'

Lucy had it all worked out. 'Look,' she said, nodding towards the laptop screen. 'There's a 24-hour telephone number for the company. I'm going to try it now.'

Lucy punched in the number on her mobile and waited for the call to be answered. She heard a recorded message, which gave lots of options. Lucy listened patiently until the option to speak to a real person was given. She pressed the number six on her phone.

And then she waited. And waited. The minutes passed as a song about sailing played over and over, until Lucy felt she knew all the words herself.

Finally she gave up. 'There's no one there,' she said to Rose. 'Or if there is, they're asleep. We'll try again in the morning. There's bound to be someone there then.'

'I hope so,' Rose said.

'It's the only thing I can think of to do.' Lucy sighed. 'We'll get through to them and say that Sarah Hammond's daughter needs to see her urgently. That's perfectly true, isn't it?'

Rose nodded. 'But what if they say that you can't meet her? They might just refuse.'

'Then I'll tell them it's an emergency,' Lucy replied. 'They'll have to let me see her.'

Rose's eyes widened. 'Cool,' she whispered. 'Totally cool!'

'We need to check the train times,' Lucy said, her fingers tapping lightly on the keyboard.

Studying routes and timetables, they plotted their journey into the middle of the city and then onwards to London Waterloo Station, where they would catch the train to Southampton.

'Docklands Light Railway, tube, then main line to Southampton. Easy,' Lucy said as she noted down the final details. 'We'll get up early and...' She stopped speaking and stared at Rose.

'What's wrong?' Rose asked. 'I can get up early, no problem. I'm always the first one up at our house.'

Lucy shook her head. 'Money,' she said. 'I don't have enough money to get myself to Southampton, never mind both of us.'

Rose smiled. 'Oh, don't worry about money. I've got lots of cash and my bank card if I run out. I can get us to Southampton, no worries.'

'Rose, I can't let you do that,' Lucy said.

'You most definitely can.' Rose grinned.

'But—'

'No argument,' Rose said. 'You're the best friend anyone could ever have and you're always doing things for me, not to mention putting up with all my moans and groans.'

Lucy smiled. 'I don't really mind your moaning and groaning. And I'll pay you back the money, I promise.'

'I don't want you to pay me back. I don't care about the money,' Rose said. 'It's my turn to do something for you and I really, really want to. So let me, please?'

'All right,' Lucy said, nodding. 'Thank you, Rose. I'll never forget this.'

'Me neither,' Rose answered. 'It's totally cool.' She thought for a moment. 'There is one thing that worries me big time though.'

'What's that?'

Rose frowned. 'Your dad.'

'I know,' Lucy said. 'It's worrying me, too. But we'll sort out everything afterwards.' She checked her watch. 'We'd better get some sleep while we can. I'll set my alarm.'

Nineteen

Despite saying that getting up early was no problem, Rose had to be shaken out of a deep slumber by Lucy. And when she finally opened her eyes, she groaned and went to turn over, saying that she simply had to have just ten more minutes because she was in the middle of a wonderful dream and she would never forgive herself if she didn't find out how it ended.

But Lucy wanted to get going before anyone else was up and about, because she just knew that her intentions would be written all over her face and that questions would be asked. So she dragged the reluctant Rose from her bed and bundled her off to the bathroom. They washed and dressed quickly and quietly and then slipped out of the back door without waking anyone.

The morning was cold and grey; a drizzly rain filled the air. All the excitement and drama of their late-night planning had drained away by the time they stepped wearily on to the first of the trains they would travel on that day.

Rose slumped in the corner seat of the empty carriage and closed her eyes. Lucy sat opposite and stared from the window, deep in thought, as the train moved slowly above the quiet streets of East London.

Soon, the giant arenas of the Olympic Park loomed into view. Even in the rain, the place looked magnificent and Lucy stared in wonder at the Aquatics Centre, just as she always did whenever she saw it.

Briefly, she thought back to her races of the previous day. Already they seemed so long ago, but she smiled, knowing that her performances had taken her that much closer to winning a place at the London 2012 Games.

She wondered how much her life would have changed by the time the Games arrived. In the corner, Rose muttered in her sleep and then turned towards the window, ending up with her nose squashed against the glass.

Lucy knew that when her parents got up, they might be surprised but not worried that she and Rose had gone out so early. They often went out together on Lucy's training-free day, sometimes to an early-morning Sunday market and sometimes to meet other friends.

There was plenty of time before Lucy would have to make the phone call home, explaining exactly what she was doing. But she was not looking forward to her dad's reaction when she finally made that call.

The train crept into the eastern edge of the city where Lucy hauled the sleepy Rose to her feet and they got off and rode the escalator down to the London Underground.

Rose sat quietly and stared blankly ahead as the tube train rumbled noisily through the tunnels and screeched to a standstill at each station. Soon, they changed from one line to another.

The walk through long corridors from one platform to another took quite a few minutes because of Lucy's disability and she found herself sighing with irritation.

'What?' Rose asked. She had hardly said a word since leaving Newham.

'I just wish I could walk as quickly as you,' Lucy snapped.

Rose shrugged and plodded on, still not wide awake. 'I wish I could swim as fast as you.'

They took the second tube train, arrived at Waterloo, and finally emerged onto the sprawling concourse of the station, with its numerous platforms, echoing announcements and arriving and departing trains.

Lucy stared up at the giant departures board. 'Now,' she said, 'which platform is it for Southampton?'

'Never mind about that,' Rose said. 'We've got plenty of time before our train leaves. And I need some breakfast.'

Rose was much more talkative after a huge breakfast of orange juice and blueberry muffins. Lucy hardly ate a thing; she was much too nervous at what the day would bring.

Once breakfast was over, they made their way to Platform 16 where the Southampton train stood waiting. They climbed aboard and found that many of the seats were already occupied, so the girls passed through several carriages until they found one that was less full.

They settled into comfortable seats and waited for the train to leave.

'Once we get out of London I'll make the phone calls,' Lucy said.

Rose raised her eyebrows. 'Rather you than me.'

Lucy nodded. 'I'll call the cruise company first. Then we'll know for certain that I can see Sarah before I call my dad to let him know what's happening.'

'Last night you were certain that you'd get to see Sarah,' said Rose.

Lucy nodded again and thought to herself that last night she'd felt much more confident about everything. But this morning a few doubts had begun to creep in. She took out Sarah's letter and read it through again. 'Do you know,' she said to Rose as she carefully refolded the precious sheets of paper, 'Sarah never once mentions my cerebral palsy in the letter.'

'Why should she?' Rose said with a shrug of her shoulders. 'It doesn't make any difference, does it?'

Lucy smiled. 'No.'

The train continued to fill up and a large, elderly lady squeezed herself into the seat next to Rose. She took a Sunday newspaper from her bag, raised it up and opened it to read, hiding herself completely from Lucy's view.

Finally, the guard's voice came over the loudspeaker announcing that they were about to start their journey and listing all the stations that they would call at. Southampton was one of the last stops.

At last, the train slowly edged out of the station and the girls gazed through the window, glimpsing the same sights that Sarah had seen a day earlier.

After ten minutes or so, Lucy took out her mobile phone and the phone number of the cruise company. 'I'd better not leave it any longer,' she said.

Rose lifted her hands to show Lucy that the first two fingers on both were firmly crossed. 'Good luck,' she breathed.

Lucy punched in the number and got through almost instantly to the same recorded message she'd heard the night before. Again, she went for for the option offering her the chance to speak to a real person.

Just like before, she waited. Then, just like before, the same music began. Lucy looked over at Rose. 'It's that song again,' she said with a shrug of her shoulders.

The seconds turned to minutes and Lucy began to think that no one would ever answer her call, when suddenly the music disappeared with a click and a woman's voice came on the line. 'Sorry to keep you waiting,' she said. 'How can I help you?'

Lucy took a deep breath. She had been rehearsing in her head what she would say next. 'Hello,' she said confidently. 'My name is Lucy Chambers and I need to get a message to Sarah Hammond who works for your company. She's my mother and I have to see her today, before she leaves on a cruise. It's very, very urgent, so please can you help me?'

The open newspaper opposite Lucy slowly sank downwards until the eyes of the elderly lady appeared. She stared with sudden interest at the girl sitting opposite, as if waiting for her conversation to continue.

'Yes, that's right. Her name's Sarah Hammond,' Lucy said, turning towards the window to escape the lady's stare.

The woman on the phone, who told Lucy her name was Michelle was friendly and helpful. Michelle said that she would make certain Sarah got Lucy's message and also that it would be possible for her to leave the ship so that they could meet.

But when Lucy told her what time the train stopped at Southampton, Michelle sounded concerned. 'Mmm,' she said. 'It doesn't give you a lot of time to get from the station to the port *and* see your mother. She has to be back on board the ship long before it actually sails. It's the same for all the passengers and the crew.'

'But I have to see her,' Lucy said, beginning to feel worried. 'It's my only chance for such a long time.'

'We'll do everything we can,' Michelle said. She took Lucy's mobile number and gave her directions to the right dock gate. If there was time, she would meet Sarah in the departures lounge on the quayside.

'Thank you so, so much,' Lucy said as she ended the call.

The lady in the seat opposite let the newspaper sink even lower. She smiled kindly at Lucy. 'I'm sure you'll get to see her,' she said.

Twenty

Lucy decided that she would go somewhere a little more private to make her call home.

The lady with the newspaper had suddenly started acting like an old friend and wanted to know all the details about Lucy and her frantic journey to meet her mother.

'Fascinating,' said the lady after Lucy explained as much as she was prepared to reveal. 'But what about your family? How do they feel about you travelling all this way to see your mother?'

'They don't actually know yet.'

The lady's eyes widened in delight. 'Really?'

'I'm going to call my dad now,' Lucy said. 'To explain.'

'Thrilling,' the lady said, settling back into her seat, as if eagerly awaiting the next phone call. 'Well, don't let me stop you.' She looked disappointed when Lucy said that she would go to the end of the carriage to make her call because it was quieter there.

'Oh, don't mind me, dear,' the lady said. 'I won't listen in.'

'No, I think it might be a difficult call,' Lucy said. 'My dad could be a bit upset so I want to speak to him on my own.'

The lady nodded. 'I understand. And you're very considerate.' She turned to Rose. 'I'll just chat with your friend here and you can tell us all about it when you get back. Good luck.'

As Lucy got up, she caught Rose's fleeting look. She could tell that her friend was silently asking her to be as quick as she possibly could. But Lucy feared that the call might take some time.

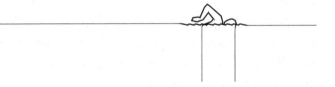

Lucy wasn't surprised when Mia answered the phone.

'Where are you?' she asked. 'Why did you go out so early? And why didn't you take me with you? I never get to go anywhere.'

'I'll explain later,' Lucy said patiently. 'But I need to speak to Dad now.'

'He's not here.'

'Oh,' Lucy said. She hadn't counted on this. 'Where is he?'

'He's gone to the garage to get petrol.'

For a moment, Lucy thought about saying that she would call back, but she knew this would worry Jo. 'Let me speak to Mum, then.'

'What do you want to talk to Mum about?'

'*Mia!* Please – I have to talk to Mum.'

'Oh, all right. But it's not fair. You never want to talk to me.'

Lucy heard Mia thud across the room and hand over the phone. Then Jo came on line.

'Hello, love,' she said. 'We thought you'd be back by now. Where are you?'

Lucy took a deep breath. 'It's a long story, Mum.'

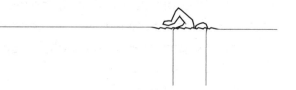

Jo listened without interrupting as Lucy told her everything. And when the entire story was told, she simply said, 'I knew all along that it would be best if you saw Sarah.'

'Are you cross with me about what I'm doing?'

Lucy heard Jo's slight laugh. 'A little bit, but I do understand why you're doing it. I'm quite impressed, too. It must have taken quite a lot of sorting out last night. And I thought you two had gone straight to sleep.'

'I didn't want to deceive you and Dad, but I knew that he wouldn't have let me come today.'

'I don't know about that,' Jo said. 'Maybe he would have allowed it, if you'd told him how much you wanted to see Sarah. You know that I'll have to tell him when he gets back, don't you?'

'Of course,' Lucy said. 'I was going to tell him myself. I told Mia that I wanted to talk to Dad.' She hesitated for a moment. 'But actually, Mum, I'm really glad that I've spoken to you.'

'Me too, love,' Jo said. 'Look, I'll explain it all to your dad and we'll speak again later, eh?'

'That'd be great,' Lucy said, feeling very relieved and grateful that her mum was so understanding.

'I hope it goes well with Sarah,' Jo said. 'I truly do. For both of you.'

'Mum, you know I—'

'You don't have to say anything else, Lucy,' Jo said quickly. 'I know how you feel and you know I feel, don't you?'

'I do, Mum,' Lucy said. 'Love you.'

The elderly lady had completely forgotten about her newspaper. She looked up in anticipation as Lucy returned to her seat with a smile on her face.

'How was it?' she said, before Rose had the chance to ask the same question.

'It was fine,' Lucy replied. 'I spoke to my mum. Dad wasn't in. And Mum was brilliant; she always is brilliant.'

'Oh, I'm so pleased,' the lady said. 'And while you've been away, Rose and I have been having such a nice chat, haven't we?'

Rose smiled and nodded but didn't look quite as delighted about the conversation as the elderly lady did.

'She's been telling me all about you being a wonderful swimmer and that you've broken all sorts of records and that you're almost certainly going to swim for Great Britain in the Olympic Games next year.'

'The Paralympic Games,' Lucy corrected her. 'And I'm not certain that I'll be in the team, but I hope so.'

'How wonderful! Your family must be so proud of you.'

Before Lucy could reply, her phone gave a musical chime, signalling the arrival of a text. She looked at Rose, fearing that it might be an angry message from her dad, but when she opened the text it wasn't from Tom at all. It was from Sarah.

> **Hello Lucy! I was so happy to get the message that you are on your way. I'll be waiting in the departures lounge and am really, really looking forward to meeting you.**
> **Sarah x**

Lucy smiled and showed the text to Rose, and then, because she so obviously wanted to see it too, to the elderly lady.

The lady adjusted her glasses and peered at the message, squinting as she read, and then gave Lucy a huge smile as she handed back the phone. 'I told you that you'd get to see her, didn't I?'

'You did.' Lucy laughed as she felt the excitement building inside her.

'I'd better phone my parents,' Rose said to Lucy, taking out her own mobile. 'But I'm not quite sure how I'm going to explain what we're doing.'

'Would you like me to talk to them, Rose?' the elderly lady asked. 'I used to be a teacher before I retired, you know. I'm used to talking to parents.'

Rose laughed. 'No, thanks,' she said. 'It's very kind of you, but I think I'll manage.'

As Rose spoke to her dad on the phone, Lucy sat back in her seat and gazed out of the window. So much had happened in so short a time and soon she would actually be meeting Sarah. At last. She felt excited, nervous, worried, and just a little bit sick because the butterflies that had fluttered around her chest the previous evening seemed to have turned into great, swooping eagles.

Rose finished her call and shrugged. 'He was fine. He just said to let them know when I'll be back.'

The train sped on, stopping occasionally, getting closer and closer to their destination. Then it began to slow again and Lucy thought that they must be approaching another station.

But the train came to a standstill in open countryside. For a few moments nothing happened and then the driver's voice came over the loudspeaker. 'Sorry about this, ladies and gentlemen. I'm afraid that a train up ahead has broken down. So there's going to be a bit of a delay while it's moved. Hopefully, it won't take too long.'

'Oh, no!' Lucy gasped. 'We'll never make it now. Never.'

'I don't believe it,' Rose said.

'Don't give up hope,' the elderly lady added. 'There's still time.'

Then Lucy's phone chimed at the arrival of another text. She took the phone from her pocket and opened the text. It was from Jo.

We're on our way. Don't Worry. Everything's OK with Dad. He's fine. But he wants to be there to bring you and Rose home after you've seen Sarah. Love, Mum xxx

Twenty-one

It had been a long delay. To Lucy, it felt like hours until the broken-down engine was shifted. Finally though, the driver announced that the track had been cleared and the train began to move again, swiftly picking up speed. But their arrival into Southampton was way behind schedule.

Lucy and Rose said farewell to the elderly lady, but only after she had written down her name and address on a page torn from her notebook and made Lucy promise to write to her to let her know the rest of the story.

'Goodbye and good luck!' she called as the girls hurried from the train. 'It's been the most enjoyable and interesting journey I can ever remember!'

Lucy had already sent a text to Sarah telling her that the train was delayed and that they would be late. Sarah had replied saying that she would wait for as long as was possible.

But as Lucy walked as quickly as she could down the platform, she was wondering if Sarah would be able to wait for long enough. The cruise ship would leave the port on time – they couldn't do anything to stop it. And Sarah was going to be on board.

The girls emerged from the station and launched themselves into the first taxi they saw, telling the driver their destination and urging him to please, please hurry. They fastened their seat belts, the taxi sped away and very soon they glimpsed the outlines of the huge passenger liners.

'There,' pointed Lucy excitedly, as they got closer and she spotted the name on one of the larger ships. 'There it is.' She checked her watch, knowing from Sarah's message that they had less than thirty minutes left. If they didn't get there soon, Lucy would probably not get another chance to see her mother for months.

The taxi pulled into the cruise line's departures area and while Rose paid the driver with what remained of her cash, Lucy clambered from the vehicle and went searching for the entrance to the building.

But there were signs everywhere, each one pointing to a different entry point, and as the precious seconds ticked by, Lucy looked frantically from one to another, searching for the right door.

'Lucy?'

She stopped and turned slowly towards the sound of the voice that had called to her. There, just a few metres away, stood Sarah.

For a few moments, neither of them moved. Lucy could see the tears in her mother's eyes and as they both edged hesitantly forward, she felt a single tear trickle down her own cheek.

And then, without Lucy realising how it had even happened, they were hugging each other tightly.

They were still locked in the embrace when Rose came running up. 'Oh, good,' she said, beaming. 'You found her.'

There was so little time. Lucy and Sarah both had so much that they wanted to say, but finding the right words was difficult. They sat at a table in the departures lounge, alone apart from Rose, who sat a few tables away. She was flicking through a magazine and trying her very best not to listen in to the conversation.

Lucy told Sarah about the journey and the broken-down train and that Tom and Jo were driving down to pick her up. They talked about swimming and school and about Sarah's job. The words they said to each other didn't seem important; the main thing was that they were speaking together, for the first time. That was all that mattered.

'I'm so glad you came,' Sarah said.

Lucy nodded. 'So am I.'

'There isn't really time to talk about the past now – about everything that happened.'

'We don't need to,' Lucy said. 'It's much more important to talk about the future.'

'I'm not sure how long I'll be away,' Sarah said. 'It could be for more than two months.'

'I'll still be here when you get back.' Lucy laughed. 'Well, not exactly here, in the departures lounge. But I will be in Newham.'

Sarah smiled. 'Perhaps you could come and visit me in Putney, when I get back.'

'I'd like that.' Lucy nodded.

They were silent for a few moments, both knowing that no words could really capture the emotions they were feeling.

'I looked the cruise up, on the Internet,' Lucy said. 'It sounds amazing. All those exciting places...'

Sarah nodded. 'We may get the chance to swim with dolphins when we reach the Caribbean.'

'Really?' Lucy said, so loudly that Rose looked up from her magazine and smiled.

'If we're lucky enough to find them,' Sarah said.

'I've always wanted to swim with dolphins,' Lucy said.

'Then, you will. I'm certain you will.' Sarah smiled at

her daughter. 'Maybe one day, you and I could—?'

The door at the end of the departures lounge opened and a man in uniform looked in. 'Sarah, we need to get on board. Sorry to rush you, but we really do need to go now.'

Sarah and Lucy stood up.

'I'll let you know about the dolphins,' Sarah said, taking Lucy's hands in hers. 'I promise. But what I want more than anything from now on is to be your friend.'

They hugged each other again and Sarah kissed her daughter on the cheek. Then she quickly turned away to leave the lounge. She looked back, gave Lucy a wave and then disappeared through the door.

Tom and Jo and Mia were waiting outside when Lucy and Rose emerged from the building.

Lucy went to Tom and put her arms around him. 'I'm sorry, Dad,' she said softly.

'No, love. I'm the one who's sorry. I should never have tried to keep you and Sarah apart.' He took a deep breath. 'How was it?'

Lucy smiled and nodded. 'It was good, Dad, really

good. But do you mind if I tell you all about it later?'

'Course not, love. You must be exhausted.' He turned to Rose. 'And you, too.'

'Not really,' Rose said. 'It's all been totally, totally cool.'

As they walked towards the car park, Lucy squeezed Jo's hand tightly. She tried to speak, but somehow the words just wouldn't come.

Jo glanced towards her daughter. 'I know, love,' she said softly. 'I know.'

Twenty-two

SIX WEEKS LATER

The postcard was waiting for Lucy when she got home from training. On the front photograph, two dolphins leapt majestically from the sun-kissed ocean, sprays of glistening water trailing in their wake.

Lucy's heart was racing as she turned the postcard over to read Sarah's now familiar writing.

Hi Lucy,

I swam with dolphins today! It was so wonderful and they were so beautiful.

But seeing you swim at London 2012 would be even more amazing. And I know that I will.

Lots of love,
Sarah

xx

Lucy Chambers
1 Coronation Walk
London
E6 7GP

Twenty-three

Golden girl, Lucy Chambers, will spearhead Great Britain's charge for precious metal in the fast-approaching London 2012 Paralympic Games.

Lucy, 15, who comes from Newham, will be among the favourites for gold in both the 200m and 400m Freestyle events in her classification.

Great performances in the Paralympic trials, followed by a series of even more impressive swims, virtually guaranteed Lucy's place, which was confirmed at the selection meeting last night.

Also selected for the ParalympicsGB team are:

Sarah looked up from the newspaper with tears in her eyes. She picked up the pair of scissors resting on the table and carefully cut the article from the page.

'Another one for the scrapbook,' she said proudly. 'That's my girl.'

Official London 2012 novels
Collect the series

Parallel lines

Blessed with twin talents, Sam Warder appears to have it all. A lightning-fast scrum-half on the rugby pitch, he also performs feats of strength and agility on the parallel bars. But the London 2012 Games are approaching and Sam is at a crossroads. Flying in the face of peer pressure, he chooses Gymnastics as his sport. And then the threatening text messages begin... Can Sam hold fast to his Olympic odyssey in a school where rugby is a religion?

ISBN 978-1-84732-750-5 • £5.99

Running in her shadow

A gifted track and field athlete, Megan Morgan has all the makings of an Olympic superstar. Whether sprinting, jumping or hurdling, her body moves like quicksilver and her sporting dreams look set to become reality. Backing Megan all the way is her determined mother. A promising athlete in her youth, she will not rest until her daughter competes for Team GB. But where is the line between love and obsession? And how much pressure can Megan withstand?

ISBN 978-1-84732-763-5 • £5.99

Wheels of fire

Rory Temu is unstoppable on his battered BMX. Weaving and dodging though the Edinburgh streets, there's no obstacle he won't tackle. Such brilliance on a bike could take Rory far – maybe even as far as the Olympic Games. But a gang on the streets has been watching closely, and the members have their own plans for Rory's talents. Rory has a gift and he intends to use it, but can he keep his balance over such rough terrain?

ISBN 978-1-84732-813-7 • £5.99

Deep waters

Lucy Chambers lives to swim. Tipped as a potential Paralympian, she has watched the Aquatics Centre rise up near her London home and hopes to make a real impression there in 2012. But the ripples of Lucy's success have reached her mother, Sarah, who left her soon after she was born. Both mother and daughter share a passion for swimming – but is now the right time to start sharing in each other's lives? For Lucy, the waters have never been deeper...

ISBN 978-1-84732-764-2 • £5.99